Song of the Day

After growing up in Thane all his life, Preet moved to the United States when he was eighteen to study at the University of California, Los Angeles. Navigating the feeling of being homesick led him to write his first book, *Song of the Day*, titled after an old ritual he followed with a friend—exchanging a song close to you every day, sometimes over chai or a long walk. Now twenty-four, Preet lives between New York and Mumbai, working as a consultant. Balancing everyday life, he continues to pursue his lifelong creative outlets of writing and making music.

Song of the Day

STORIES

PREET MODI

Published by Westland Books, a division of Nasadiya Technologies Private Limited, in 2024

No. 269/2B, First Floor, 'Irai Arul', Vimalraj Street, Nethaji Nagar, Alapakkam Main Road, Maduravoyal, Chennai 600095

Westland and the Westland logo are the trademarks of Nasadiya Technologies Private Limited, or its affiliates.

Copyright © Preet Modi, 2024

Preet Modi asserts the moral right to be identified as the author of this work.

ISBN: 9789360457952

10 9 8 7 6 5 4 3 2 1

This is a work of fiction. Names, characters, organisations, places, events and incidents are either products of the author's imagination or used fictitiously.

All rights reserved

Typeset by Mukul

Printed at Thomson Press (India) Ltd

No part of this book may be reproduced, or stored in a retrieval system, or transmitted in any form or by any means, electronic, mechanical, photocopying, recording, or otherwise, without express written permission of the publisher.

To my family, friends and my language teachers

In loving memory of Kaval ma'am

Contents

Chasing Cars	1
Budapest	16
Tum Jab Paas	26
Candy Says	40
Gulaabi	50
Iktara	59
Blackbird	67
Thirteen	78
The Little Things You Do	97

Chasing Cars

K ALKI DIPPED HER FEET IN THE COLD POOL WATER AND SLOWLY swayed them back and forth in waves. The soft splashing sound playfully flirted with the silence of the wound-down August night. A curtain of mist had enveloped the place that periodically fluttered each time a strong wind blew, breaking the spell of calm that pervaded the air. Amidst the occasional soft rustle of trees, she sat there staring at her palms under the yellow lamplights as small droplets of rain settled on them. Wet leaves and washed-up dirt littered the beige poolside floor. She looked around to check if someone was watching her, then unsteadily pulled out a cigarette and smoked it whole.

'Do you mind if I sit here?' a boy's voice cut in right as she was about to light another one.

Song of the Day

'Sure. I don't own the place,' Kalki replied indifferently.

'Thank you,' he spoke softly as he set down a black leather bag between them and sat about ten inches away from her. Kalki turned her head at an angle to get a better look at him.

'We've met before, haven't we?' she asked with a faint sense of recognition.

'We have. Once. I'm Kabir … a friend of Tara's. You're Kalki, right? She always speaks so fondly of you,' he said in a broken rush.

'She talks a lot about you too. I'm sorry I didn't recognise you initially. Your glasses—they're different from what I remember.'

'That's okay,' Kabir said as he took off his shoes and dipped his feet into the water. 'It's a strange night.'

An awkward silence followed. The ripples caused by their movements cancelled each other out before they could reach the other end of the pool. Some of the mist around them had started to lift and the night sky was growing clear again. As the moonlight shone over their bodies, an uneasiness ran between them. Kabir felt the cold pool water seep between his toes.

'Tara only brought the most special people to this place,' Kalki said, finally breaking the silence. A distinct hesitation was etched in her voice.

'I know. It's the only place I could think of coming to,' Kabir replied. He reached out to pick up a fallen flower from the ground and plucked its petals apart one at a time.

'Me too. I came here to be alone. Away from everyone,' she sighed.

'I'm sorry that I'm here.' He collected the broken petals and held them tightly in his fist.

'Please don't apologise. Maybe it's better to be with someone tonight. Besides, in a way we share this place now. It's important to come here. For her sake …'

'How are you dealing with it?' Kabir looked at Kalki desperately as the petals slowly slipped out of his hand and gently landed in the water. Another drizzle of rain poured down on them.

'I don't know. I just can't process it,' she replied.

'Me neither,' Kabir said after some thought as he slowly lifted his feet from the pool. He hunched and planted his head on his knees. 'I saw the police cars on my way here. I didn't believe it until then. How could she just—just die like that? It just doesn't feel real …'

'I was talking to her only a few hours ago,' Kalki's voice trailed off into a murmur. Another brief pause settled over the conversation. Both of them seemed to be gathering their composure.

'How did it happen?' Kabir asked feebly after some time.

'Nobody knows for sure. It seems like she was on her balcony and slipped over the unguarded railing. The police don't want to question anyone yet. Everyone's in a state of shock.'

'It was going to be her seventeenth birthday in a few days.'

'I know.' Kalki pulled out another cigarette and let it sit between her lips. 'We're all just sixteen and seventeen. Nobody was prepared for this.' Kabir stared into the distance at the drops of rain falling through the unguarded sky.

Song of the Day

'Want a smoke?' Kalki asked. 'It helps.'

'No, thanks, I don't do that,' he replied without looking at her.

'Please don't judge me for this. I started a little early. But give it a year, and I think you'll start smoking too.' She lit up her cigarette and took a puff. A thin, long trail of smoke rose from her mouth.

'Why do you think so?'

'Doesn't almost everyone?'

Kabir was silent again. Tiny flecks of ash flew in various directions. The mellow sound of Kalki smoking sustained in the air like a bleak monotone.

'I think I'm going to go now,' she announced once the cigarette had burnt itself out. 'We might see each other here again.'

'I guess so. Do you need a ride?'

'No, I'm meeting my boyfriend.'

'Okay then. I think I'm going to stay here for a few more minutes,' he said as he took off his glasses.

'Okay. Please take care of yourself.'

'I will.'

Kalki put an arm around Kabir and held him affectionately, then picked herself up and walked away from the pool. She glanced back at him once, and he waved at her. She waved back and continued walking through a patch of wet grass. Brown mud stains settled on her off-white shoes, and she felt an unbearable sense of grief come over her. The sight of Kabir waving at her by the pool was stuck on a loop in her mind. Some parts of the image felt like they were covered in stains.

Once Kalki had left, Kabir could think of Tara more clearly. The realisation of loss crept into his mind, like cold water seeping in between toes. In his pocket was a note that she had slipped to him during the farewell they had given their seniors. Kabir had borrowed his brother's suit for the night, and Tara was wearing her mother's sari. And in their slightly misfitting clothes, they had clicked numerous photographs together in the hope of preserving that night. At the end of the party, as everyone was leaving, Tara had held Kabir's hand and given him a small piece of paper.

As he stared at the note now, Kabir was unable to get himself to cry. Eventually, he put it away without opening it and his gaze shifted back to the pool. The petals that he had been holding earlier had drifted away to different parts of the water. He thought about Tara and their time together as he spotted the petals one by one. It seemed like those memories too would scatter and gradually decay if he wasn't careful. Slowly, he would start forgetting fine details about her. The process seemed inevitable, yet the only thing that made sense was to preserve everything that he felt for her.

While he struggled to make sense of things, the rain halted at once. It felt like time had come to a halt too, but then, a guard appeared and told Kabir that it was time for the pool to shut, and he reluctantly agreed to leave. As Kabir walked away from the place though, he felt that he had found a way to resolve the conflict inside him. He made a promise to himself to always carry Tara in his thoughts. To think about her every day.

The First Anniversary

'I didn't expect you to be here,' Kabir said as he spotted Kalki sitting by herself at the pool. She wore a faded floral top and denim shorts that revealed tanned legs from the summer gone by.

'Yet, you decided to get two cups of coffee?' she said with a smirk. It was not too late in the evening, and sunlight lingered in shimmering puddles over the surface of the pool. A few kids splashed about in the water in their nylon swimwear and smooth latex caps.

'Just in case I needed more than one,' Kabir explained.

'Fair enough,' she replied and motioned for him to sit beside her. Kabir did so and handed her one of the paper cups he was holding.

'Thank you. How are you doing?' she asked as she blew at the bubbles in her coffee before taking a sip.

'I'm okay. What about you?'

'Me too. How's life after school treating you?' she asked.

'It's not that different. I started going to college a month back. It's a place near Churchgate Station, so I commute by train every day. It takes a little over an hour one way, and I need to change lines once in the middle, but I'm getting used to it.'

'That sounds tiring. Have you made any new friends? Anyone you can travel with?'

'I've got to know a few people, but no one I can truly connect with,' he replied gloomily.

'I'm sure you just need more time.'

'Maybe. What about you?'

'I'm going to attend a law school in Pune. Our first term starts at the end of the month, and I'm really excited.'

'That sounds fun.'

'I hope it is,' she said, secretly crossing her fingers behind her back. The act went unnoticed as Kabir was looking at a flock of pigeons that was drinking water at the edge of the pool. Their light-grey plumes stuck out from slits in the plastic drainage. Suddenly, a pair of twelve-year-olds charged at the pigeons at full speed, causing them to startle. In an instant, the flapping of wings filled the air as the pigeons swiftly took flight. A fit of gleeful laughter echoed through the air, and the kids jumped into the pool with a big splash to celebrate. Once inside, they finally grew quiet again and interlaced their little fingers together to make a promise.

'Can I tell you something?' Kabir asked as he looked away from the kids and focused on an arbitrary point in the water where bubbles of air were rising up in a continuous stream.

'Sure, go on,' Kalki replied.

'A few days before Tara passed away, she told me about a dream that she had,' he started. 'It was nighttime, and the sky was filled with an equal number of red and blue stars.

She told me that she couldn't picture it anymore, but she was sure that what she had seen was the most beautiful pattern in the sky. In the dream, she was trying to take a picture of the pattern because she wanted to preserve it. But something or the other—an object or a person—would always obstruct her view and spoil the photograph. She kept trying, but no matter where she went, she couldn't get a proper shot.'

'That's a very strange dream.'

'It is. I keep thinking about it for some reason. What do you think it meant?'

'That's hard to say. Maybe something like we shouldn't try to hold onto moments but live through them. Sounds a little clichéd though.'

'That's not a bad interpretation.'

'But you know, maybe it didn't mean anything at all. Not all dreams have a significance.'

'You're right about that,' Kabir murmured and let out a soft whistle of air, repeating the phrase to himself. He pushed his socks down to his ankles and got up at once. 'It's too loud here. Let's sit somewhere else,' he suggested as he discarded his empty cup into a bin.

They picked out a white iron bench in a garden next to the pool. Small shrubs hung in an arc over their heads as they settled in. The sun dipped below the horizon, and drops of evening dew scattered across the dark green bed of grass. Vine-covered stone posts lined either side of a central bird bath that had filled up with rainwater. A soft beam of light fell on its surface, making it glow like a small sunlit pond.

'Want a smoke?' Kabir asked as he produced a box of cigarettes.

'You're full of surprises,' Kalki laughed. 'Do you think Tara would feel bad if she saw us smoking? She would always scold me for it like a mother.'

'Should we not then?' he asked, almost putting the box away.

'Let's just share one,' she replied, and Kabir quickly lit a Dunhill from his pack and took a few short drags.

'So, are you still dating your boyfriend?' he asked as he passed her the cigarette.

'That guy from last year? Oh no. I stopped seeing him. I'm with someone else now.'

'Oh, okay.' He tapped his foot nervously against the bench's metal leg.

'What? Do you think I'm shallow for having dated a lot of guys?' she asked irritably as she ashed her cigarette over the grass.

'Why would I? That doesn't say anything about you.'

'Of course, it doesn't.' She scoffed at the idea for a moment. 'I'm sorry, I have a habit of thinking people get the wrong impression about me. You're not like that though, I know. You're a better person than that.'

'I'm sorry for anything that bothered you. But what makes you feel that way?'

'It's not a big deal or anything. Do you really want to know?'

'Yes,' Kabir nodded.

Song of the Day

'So, I went through seeing a few guys in school. But something or the other happened and things didn't work out. There were boys in my grade who dated quite a few girls too. But for some reason people started talking about me ... in a bad way.' She paused to take a long drag from their shared cigarette. 'At our school farewell, someone wrote my number on a wall in the boys' toilet. You get what I'm saying, right? Anyway, I found out from a friend. Somehow, everyone else also heard about it and people kept looking at me strangely throughout the night.'

'That is such a horrible thing—I'm so sorry. Did you talk to someone about it?'

'Who was I supposed to talk to? It doesn't matter. As I told you, it's not a big deal. School's over now and I will be far away from that place. Besides, I'm very happy in my current relationship. His name's Shaun. It's premature, but I really think we could go a long way.'

'That's really sweet.'

'It is, I know. Here, you can have the rest,' she said as she handed him the fag end of the cigarette and got up to dump her coffee. The cup seemed like it was halfway full as it fell with a dull thud, and Kabir guessed that she probably didn't like the blend that he had chosen.

'I think Shaun's here to pick me up. We're going on a ride on his motorcycle. Is it okay if I leave?' she announced when she returned. Kabir decided that it was a good time for him to go too. He stamped out the Dunhill cigarette with his off-white shoe and walked with her towards the exit. The children in the pool had left by then and the violent mischief in the air had subsided.

'Let's meet here again next year,' Kalki said jokingly as they eventually split up to go different ways.

'Let's meet here again,' Kabir repeated with an uncertain smile, and Kalki turned to leave without any other gesture of farewell. He watched her as she mounted Shaun's motorcycle and disappeared into the traffic. Then he walked back to his car and started driving to nowhere in particular. Iron Maiden blasted from the speakers as he drove, and his thoughts raced through corridors of memory recounting his own farewell. He had lurked alone in the dark corners of the party hall that night, purposefully avoiding friends who he couldn't envision being in touch with for more than two years at best. Occasionally somebody would spot him standing alone and drag him in to dance, but he would quickly draw himself away at the first opportunity. Those few hours of celebration had passed slowly for him like a long, sleepless night.

Circling in the dull recollection of that night, Kabir came to a halt and abruptly turned off the music. He opened Tara's note and placed it carefully under the car's interior light. The softened paper seemed like it would tear as it grazed against his thumb. He could still feel the warmth of her fingers linked to his palm when she had handed the note to him. The delicate glow of the gemstone ring she used to wear to ward off evil spirits lingered faintly in his memory.

'At our farewell, will you dance with me?'

He read the question to himself several times, then carefully folded the paper back along the creases and started driving again. In the end, he had graduated without her.

∽

The Second Anniversary

A heavy burst of rain poured against Kabir's black polyester raincoat as he walked through puddles of ankle-deep water. Over the last year, he had started skipping college on most days and had spent his time sitting alone at cheap coffee houses doing nothing in particular. Today was one of those rare occasions when he had managed to attend his lectures. After his classes had ended for the day, he had felt a strong urge not to go home. He had taken a slow train on his way back and then boarded an empty bus from the station. Inside the bus, the rhythmic clinks of metal straps swinging back and forth kept reminding him of how silent their school was the day after Tara's accident. He made up his mind to get off near her apartment and visit the pool again.

As Kabir walked to the place, he wondered whether he would see Kalki again. After all, she had suggested that they meet again even if she was only half serious. When he finally reached the pool though, the place was completely desolate. He glanced at the nearby garden and noticed that the bench where he and Kalki had sat down a year ago was no longer there, replaced by dirt and an overgrowth of grass. Residential lights blurred in the distance beyond, accompanied by an unwavering gust sweeping through the air. Under the rain, the water in the pool rippled and seemed to fold and unfold in an endless motion.

Kabir waited for a long time, but Kalki never showed up. When the rain finally eased, he sat alone at the edge of the pool and smoked in the darkness. After a while, he cried a lot, but eventually, it felt okay. He felt a strange sense of relief because Kalki hadn't shown up. Maybe she was out somewhere—on the back seat of Shaun's motorcycle perhaps—in love and able to forget. The thought was reassuring to him.

A few mornings ago, he had woken up earlier than usual and cried for no apparent reason. He could only remember fragments of a dream that had been playing in his mind: He was a boy in a raincoat looking at a lantern gliding across the night sky; its small light shining faintly in the air like the distant glow of a gemstone ring. And somehow when he woke up, there had been a disorienting change within him. He had felt it more clearly on his way back from college a few days later as familiar landscapes drifted past the train's windows. A strange stillness. As if the fluttering inside of an older time had grown stagnant and the back and forth swinging of metal straps had finally stopped. A realisation dawned on him, one that he had been trying to evade.

Two years ago, on a relatively calm monsoon night, Tara had died, and he had never been able to convey the true extent of his feelings towards her. He felt like he was sixteen, and now,

Song of the Day

all of a sudden, he had turned eighteen. There was no way to reconcile the years in between. A longing had enveloped him two years ago, and it had followed him everywhere he went—at swimming pools and train stations; at dirty cigarette stalls and parking lots in shopping malls. But recently, he had had a change of heart. There had been days when Tara had slipped out from his thoughts. He had made a few close friends, and there was a girl that he had developed feelings for.

A strong wind ruffled Kabir's hair, and he wondered if it was okay to break his promise to Tara. To not always keep her in his thoughts. To not think about her every day.

'What song would we dance to?' he had written back to her the night of the farewell, and she had whispered the answer to him with a hug. Kabir closed his eyes as he played *Chasing Cars* by Snow Patrol for the first time in two years. Until then, it had seemed to him that he couldn't listen to the song anymore. Tara's death had swept his heart clean of something innocent that he could no longer retrieve. The days before her death felt like a time when everything had been incredibly pure. Like a gentle morning that hadn't touched the colour of the grass yet, and one could still hold the dew between their fingertips. When she passed away, all he felt he could do anymore was try to cling on to what was left of her inside him. To desperately hold on to a place, a song and an old note that carried his only image of her handwriting. It was like one of those promises kids make by interlacing their little fingers together. The most honest childhood gesture. But no one made those promises anymore.

Chasing Cars

Kabir held on to the note tenderly while he waited for the last bits of the track to play out. As the song ended, he dipped his feet in the cold pool water and slowly swayed them back and forth in waves. A few splashes later, he smiled and left for home.

∼

Budapest

'Do you think it's weird that we never sit opposite each other?' a boy of about eighteen asked the girl seated next to him. The first trails of sunlight gently crept up to their faces, with the tender footsteps of a newlywed bride.

'That's just the way we orient ourselves with respect to the world,' she replied, sipping from her short glass of chai. A tiny cloud of smoke formed around her face. His hand grazed against her little finger as the rusty metal shutter of an old shopping centre creaked in the wind.

'Aren't you excited? You've always dreamed of going to film school,' she said as some snowflakes got crushed under the soles of her shoes.

'Why are you studying to join the civil services then? Why not literature?' He drew his hand back, away from hers.

'We come from a small town. Girls who study literature get pushed into marriage before they can finish college.'

'So, you're saying preparing for the civil services entrance is a good way to put off marriage?'

'You could say so.'

'Vaani!'

'Ishaan.'

'But you write so beautifully,' he said almost pleadingly as he looked directly at her. She lowered her gaze and smiled to herself. The sharp glow of an old yellow lightbulb dimmed as daylight settled around them.

'Will you do a photo shoot of me one day, Mr Cinematographer?' Vaani asked shyly.

'Only if you don't forget about me,' Ishaan replied as he looked up at the sky. A bonfire burning close by was warming his feet.

'You're the one moving to another country,' she said somewhat coldly.

'Today feels like the last day of winter. The season's going to turn tomorrow,' he responded after some time. 'I'm sorry.'

'As we are now, we're holding each other back,' Vaani said as she closed her eyes and placed a kiss on Ishaan's forehead. They got up from the table and stood facing each other.

'I wish I met you when I was twenty-five,' Ishaan said, wrapping his arm around Vaani's waist.

'I hope you find what you're looking for,' she replied softly. He watched her as the bonfire crackled and its embers drifted towards them before vanishing in their attempts at reaching the mesh of her fleece sweater.

'One day, if we're in a different city, and both of us aren't with anyone, let's get married,' Vaani said with a smile after a moment. Amidst the cold, white winter wind, her words fell apart like a small seashell being stepped on. Ishaan nodded his head and turned away to walk alone through the melting snow.

I first met Vaani at the Literature Club in college midway through our second year. We realised that we had joined the same coaching classes to prepare for the Civil Services Examination and quickly became good friends. We met several times during the rest of the year at small coffee shops and dingy roadside bookstores where we'd read stories by Manto and Premchand; Wodehouse and Murakami. Time passed by quickly, and when our sophomore summer finally arrived, both of us found ourselves staying back over the break. We both had our reasons for not wanting to go back home. Studying together, we figured, would make it easier to get by. And so, we decided to meet up at her apartment at 8 a.m. every day to study.

That summer, I would always wake up before sunrise and gaze out of my bedroom window, waiting for the daylight to reach me. Like a forbidden daily affair, it would tiptoe towards me, and I would steal a few fleeting moments with it. After that, I'd start my morning and take a rickshaw to go to Vaani's home. On my way, I'd make a stop to buy a packet of milk, and Vaani would use it to make chai for the both of us. Her recipe would involve crushed black pepper and powdered cardamom, their blend crafting a mix of sweetness and spice in gentle, balanced proportions. 'I always try to recreate the taste of the tea from a stall by my house,' she had once told me.

Vaani would always pour the chai out in careful, equally measured halves into two matching cups adorned with peacocks that her grandmother had left to her. We would spend twenty minutes or so listening to music and talking about things—like the songs that we'd recently discovered and new movies running at the cinema. After that, we would start studying for the day. I'd pour myself a breakfast of leftover milk and cereal to eat along. Two meals a day sufficed for Vaani, and so, she would never eat in the mornings. A tiffin service would deliver our lunch and dinner, and we would carry on with most of our day reading and making notes while taking small breaks in between. Around midnight, I would leave to go back to my place, and we would repeat our routine over the following day.

～

'Who's your favourite poet?' Vaani asked me one night as we sat in her room.

Song of the Day

'Rainer Maria Rilke,' I replied after some consideration.

'I haven't read him. Anything you'd recommend?'

'His letters,' I smiled.

She seemed to make a mental note of my words as she switched on a night lamp and put on her red reading glasses. The glossy metal frame hung loosely on her nose as she opened a thin leather-bound book in front of her. She'd often do that—take off her moccasins, slip into the bed and read out poetry by Rumi or Plath; only the lines that struck her. Music would often play out loud, and she would tap her pen along to the rhythm of the songs, then spin it around in a circle like a lunar cycle being completed.

'It's funny, I've run out of poems today. Do you mind if I talk to you?' she asked me all of a sudden.

'Of course. We can talk,' I replied as I collected some scattered loose pages I had been writing on. I glanced at the calendar hung up on the wall behind her. It was the first day of June and summer was almost about to end.

'You know, I was thinking today, it's amazing how little of post-Independence history is taught to us,' Vaani remarked as she removed her glasses and gently placed them aside. *Budapest* by George Ezra played warmly in the background.

'Do you think there's a reason for it?'

'I'm not sure,' she replied and started thinking hard about it. 'Do you know George Ezra never went to Budapest? He missed his train to go there,' she said after a while, passing seamlessly on to the next thought on her mind.

'So, he wrote a song after a place he had never seen?'

'Isn't that interesting?'

'You know, I enjoy talking to you about these things,' I said softly as I turned my gaze to her bedside window. Its glass panelling was covered by light splatters of dust, and tiny scratches, etched over time.

'I do too,' she replied with a smile. 'Do you want to sit by the windowsill?'

'Yes, let's do that during our next break,' I smiled back at her. We studied for a few more hours after that until it was almost midnight. I got up a few minutes before our usual time to make some chai and carefully carried the cups back into the room.

We climbed out the window, and perched ourselves on a sill. Faintly visible power lines stretched into the distance, and there was an emptiness spread across the city. A faint drizzle scattered down from the clouds.

'Do you believe in palm reading?' Vaani asked me as she collected some raindrops in her hand.

'Not really. Do you?'

'I'm not sure. I used to compare palm lines with my friends when we were kids. We would think of them as lines of fate.'

'Did you ever learn anything interesting?'

'Nothing that I can remember. But it all seemed true back then,' she said as she gazed into the distance at cars drifting through the city.

'Maybe as we grow up, we realise how little of what we know is certain,' I said after some thought.

Song of the Day

'Or maybe growing up just reduces the possibilities we can imagine. I think I'm more boring as an adult than what I was as a kid.' Vaani stared at the blue tin roof above us that would funnel rainwater into thin streams flowing down through the air during monsoon downpours. Her soft white top stuck to her chest, and, for the first time, I wondered about the colour of her eyes.

'Do you remember I told you how Ishaan and I parted?' Vaani asked me suddenly, almost in a hushed tone.

I looked at her and nodded my head.

'That wasn't the end of it. A year later, we met at a cafe on a summer evening and told each other that we would make things work. But a few weeks later, I went on a date with someone else.'

'Why?'

'Why I went on that date? I don't know. I just couldn't bring myself to face the past again. Since then, we've only been sending each other these things in the post to avoid talking.' She pulled out an envelope with a cat symbol from her pocket and loosely held it in her palm. 'Ishaan and I exchange these letters every month. He sends me pictures of his favourite new places. He's always on the move, travelling from one city to another.'

'Where is he now?'

'In Prague, I reckon,' Vaani replied as she glanced at the postage stamp stuck onto the envelope. 'You know, I still remember him walking away from me as the snow around us was melting under the sun. It's almost as if the only way for us to ever be together was for me to run after him that day before the snow completely melted and tell him that we were making a mistake. Deep down, we both knew that once the snow disappeared, there could never be a way back for us. It's all in the past and it doesn't affect me anymore. But you know, sometimes …' Vaani's voice trailed off into silence.

'Did you receive another letter this month?' I asked softly.

'No …' she said as she tried to smile at me. The moonlight tenderly caressed parts of her face and for the first time, I realised I liked her voice better than mine. It made me want to hold her close to me. I drew my arm around her, and she squeezed my hand tightly like a child awakened by the sound of midnight fireworks exploding in the sky. We remained in each other's embrace for a while, the wind seeping through the small gaps between us.

'Do you want to play a game?' I asked Vaani once she looked up at me.

'What game?' she replied, gently rubbing her eyes.

'It's something we used to play as kids in school. It's called thumb fight.'

'Thumb fight?' she asked, a little amused.

'So, we hold hands while making a fist,' I said as I held her hand again. 'Then we raise our thumbs. The person who can pin the other's thumb down until a count of three wins.'

'So, you do this?' she replied as she pinned my thumb down and counted to three.

'Yes, just like that.'

'Then I won!' she declared and started laughing.

Song of the Day

It brought a broad smile to my face, and I scratched my head in defeat. After that, we played many games like Chopsticks, Hand Cricket and Atlas. And we spoke of the lives we had led before we met each other. Without either of us realising it, the night slipped away, and the rain subsided. In the fading darkness, lingering droplets clung tightly onto the edges of leaves, reminiscent of young lovers in a parting embrace.

'It's almost sunrise,' I said as the morning air struck against my face.

'You know, I like sitting beside you,' Vaani replied, and we smiled at each other. 'I'm hungry today,' she continued after a moment. 'Will you make breakfast for me?'

'Of course,' I replied and wondered if I could figure out what she liked.

I gave up on the Civil Services Examination before my first attempt. I realised it just wasn't for me. By the time we reached the end of our final year of college, I was gearing up to relocate to Mumbai and start a new life in the city. Our college hosted a small farewell for our batch, and Vaani and I talked for a long time that night. She told me that she had decided to stay back and continue preparing for the exam. After the ceremony concluded, we ended up taking a short walk together and signed each other's hand before parting ways.

～

As time passed, Vaani and I lost touch, and I never met her again after college. Back then, I had feelings for her, but I could never bring them up in any way. If I could meet her now, I still don't know whether I could bring myself to face the past again and tell her how I truly felt. Yet, as time has passed, I've realised that we both needed each other as friends more than anything else. In those strange, confusing years of early adulthood, she was my companion and my source of comfort. I'll always remember her through the rituals we formed all those years ago. All the evenings we spent visiting tiny old bookstores, hunting for that one title we wanted to read, and all the mornings when we'd drink chai together in her grandmother's cups. Most of all, I'll always remember her for the time that we spent chasing after the same dreams together.

Every year now, I scan the list of selected candidates for the civil services, hoping, one day, to find her name. And sometimes I wonder, whether in Budapest or Prague, or some other faraway city that I may never visit, Ishaan has been searching for her too.

～

Tum Jab Paas

6 'AS A KID, DID YOU EVER THINK THAT RATHER THAN US moving, it's the trees that are going backward?' Aryan asked Tanya in a tired voice. They stared outside while standing at the exit door of a train compartment. The blue haze of a gloomy winter morning brushed up against their faces.

'Sometimes, yes,' she replied as she rubbed her eyes. 'The sun's almost up now. I can't believe we were talking the whole night. We're lucky we didn't get caught by a teacher.'

'I think it was the best night of the whole trip. I'm going to miss this. Not so much school, but just this feeling right now. It's a shame there's only a few months left before we go to college.' The train swayed up and down rhythmically as it raced along the tracks.

Tum Jab Paas

'Your hair is so soft.' Tanya playfully stroked Aryan's head as she drew her face closer and pressed her nose gently against his. 'I think I really like you.'

Aryan felt his heart wallop faster than the train. He wanted to say it back, but somehow, the words got caught up in his mouth. A moment of silence settled into the air between them. Tanya drew herself back and stared at the ground. Her fingers nervously traced the fabric of her uniform.

'Tanya, it's just the timing of things—'

'It's okay, you don't have to explain yourself. I know you're going to go to college in London. I'm so proud of you,' she said, mustering a weak smile. The train rattled momentarily, producing a sharp noise that sliced through the air. Tanya almost tripped but managed to hide any traces of an imbalance.

'You'll come back to Delhi though, won't you?'

'Yes, I'll fly back every time I have a break.' There was a shiver in Aryan's voice. He attributed it to the cold air outside.

'That's good. I'm happy I'll get to see you even after school ends.' Tanya's smile widened as she spoke. Aryan felt as if he saw warm shades of pastel when he looked at her. With the right half of her hair tucked behind her ear and the left half falling in front of her eyes, the thought of the inevitable distance between them stirred an ache in the pit of his stomach. Maybe Tanya realised what Aryan felt then, for she gently drifted forward to hold him. In their embrace, Aryan whispered something into Tanya's ear, but the train's whistle shot a blaring sound, drowning it into oblivion. Though she couldn't hear what he said, the muffled tone of his voice gave away enough. They stood there in each other's arms for a while. It appeared to dull the ache in their stomachs but created a new one in their hearts.

∽

'How do you feel? Are you nervous about leaving?' Tanya asked Aryan. She was wearing a new cream sweater, and her hair was tied up behind with a black hair tie. It did an incredible job of keeping all the strands held together.

'I'm a little nervous, but mostly excited I think,' he replied as they walked around Tanya's neighbourhood. 'I've just worked so hard for this moment and it's finally here.'

'I'm excited for you too. You're going to take London by storm! I know it.'

'Well, that's the plan,' he said with a casual shrug of his shoulders.

'Should we sit down somewhere?'

Aryan nodded and they found a wooden bench nearby. Tanya sat down facing Aryan, her legs folded underneath her. He did the same. She leaned forward and playfully ran her hands through his hair.

'Your hair has grown so long. Aren't you going to cut it?' she asked, twirling his hair into curls.

'I will at some point. You know I don't like having my hair short.'

Tanya smiled when he said that. She removed her hair tie and let it hang from her fingers. The act struck Aryan as exceptionally beautiful. Just the sight of Tanya smiling with her hair open seemed to rid his heart of any imbalance. She raised her eyebrows as if to ask him what he was looking at, but Aryan coyly shook his head. She crept closer to him, used her hair tie to form a small ponytail with his hair and started laughing.

'I look great, don't I?' he asked.

'The best,' she replied, laughing even harder. It made Aryan laugh too. The sound of their laughter hung in the air for a few moments before dissipating into the static of silence.

'So, you leave tonight, huh?' Tanya asked rhetorically in a hushed tone. Aryan stared into the distance. 'You'll come back soon though, right? For winter break?' she continued with a newfound energy in her voice.

'Honestly, I don't know if I will. I wanted to tell you about it. My parents are moving back to Mumbai to live with my grandparents. So, when I get back, I'll go there. I am not sure when I'll come to Delhi again.'

Tanya crushed a dried-up leaf in her palm, creating an irregular crunching sound. She appeared engrossed in the process. 'You may not be able to come back this winter, but surely in the summer you would have enough time, right?' She let the fragments of the leaf slip out of her fist.

'I may work over the summer. I don't know where that will be, or for how long. It's all a little confusing now. I mean, I don't like the idea of not being able to come back here. But at the same time, I really want to go.'

'It's natural to feel torn between the things we love. You love Delhi, it's home. But you also love the dream you've been chasing. Love isn't singular that way. It's made up of many strands, and it becomes difficult to hold all of them together.' Aryan seemed to be trying to resolve the meaning of her words. Tanya looked at his engrossed face for a moment and got up at once. 'Come, let's go. I have an idea,' she said, her hand outstretched. He took her hand in his.

'I wanted to take my hair tie back, but you can do that too.'

He drew his hand back a little flustered, then handed her the tie from his hair. She wore it around her wrist, and they started walking again. It was late in the evening by then. Dim traces of night lights had started to emerge around them. The clouds painted a palette of orange across a gently darkening indigo sky. They walked for fifteen minutes, watching the evening sun burn out, before stopping at a small coffee stall by the edge of the Yamuna River. Tanya pulled out a neatly folded twenty-rupee note and placed an order for two espressos.

'I remember that you love street coffee,' she said, handing Aryan one of the paper cups.

'We talked about it on the train, didn't we? Is that why you got me here?'

'Of course not. We've come here for the view,' Tanya said with a burst of childlike excitement. She pointed in the distance to the figure of the Delhi Eye spinning slowly. Its reflection

Tum Jab Paas

dissolved in the water making a silver ring on the surface. 'There's a Ferris wheel like this in London too, right? Delhi and London aren't too different that way.'

Aryan took a sip of his coffee as he tried to absorb the sight in front of him. The slow motion of the wheel offered him a sense of comfort. They sat down on a ledge, letting their feet dangle above the water. 'You love Hindi music, don't you?' Aryan asked Tanya all of a sudden.

'Yes, and you don't.'

'That's not true. I actually found a song that I like. I wanted you to listen to it.' Aryan pulled out his phone and played Prateek Kuhad's *Tum Jab Paas*. The low buzz of the city's evening rush was drowned out by the sound of music. They continued to gaze at the Delhi Eye as they sipped their coffee and listened to the song. Aryan felt like he had a lot to say but was cautious not to speak, afraid that he would stain the moment with words.

Eventually, the song gently played itself out and faded away, inducing a paralysis of sorts. Aryan was the first one to recover from it. 'I must get going now,' he said with a dryness in his voice.

'Yes, I know,' Tanya replied. Her eyes felt moist. She attributed it to the cold air outside. 'My cheeks are cold, aren't they?' she asked, guiding Aryan's hand to her face.

'Yes. So are mine,' he replied with a smile.

Aryan stepped closer to her, and they held each other in a soft embrace. Tanya inhaled sharply and whispered into his ear, 'Thank you for sharing your song with me.'

'It's the song of the day,' he whispered back as he tightened his grip just a little.

When they finally let each other go, Tanya handed Aryan her hair tie which he stored safely in his wallet. Then the realisation of time took over, and they parted ways.

~

Two years later

Tanya stood at the centre of the wedding lawn, a little lost, desperately looking for her mother. Her teal sari fluttered gently in the breeze of a cold Delhi night. She ran into familiar faces occasionally as she moved from one end to another, exchanging polished greetings and indulging in idle chatter. It was what weddings in Delhi were like. There would be a huge gathering and you would always run into someone unexpected.

Unable to locate her mother, Tanya decided to take a break from her search and sat down at a table by herself. She gave her mother a call, but it went unanswered. Frustrated, she slammed the phone onto the table. A freezing gust swept against her hair, making it flow. The night had been a dull affair overall.

Tanya's parents had separated a few months ago owing to differences that they just couldn't sort out. One fight after another, they ended up uncovering a deep well of pent-up anger and hurt. Every time Tanya thought about it, she felt like she was staring into that darkness, consuming it piece by piece until it made her breathless. Social gatherings only worsened the feeling. After the news of her parents' separation broke out, everyone started behaving strangely. Some people became excessively nice and concerned, while others turned sarcastic and crude. Everyone seemed to have learnt how to speak in multiple tongues. Tanya struggled to understand why.

Another wave of cold air struck against her partially exposed back. It made her involuntarily jump to her feet and walk over to a nearby fireplace. She stretched out her hands over the flame, repeatedly opening and closing her fists. The warmth helped release some of the tension in her body. She stood by the fire comfortably for the next few minutes, rubbing her hands over her face. It restored some of the pink that had faded from her cheeks.

Tanya continued to stare at the burning planks of wood. She began pondering how the wood was slowly consuming itself just to keep others warm. She followed the trail of the smoke and wondered if that was how planks of wood cried—silently, with no traces of any tears. She hadn't arrived at an answer when she noticed a familiar figure on the other side of the fire.

Tanya had always thought that when she met Aryan again, she would recognise him instantly. However, it took her some effort to register that he was standing in front of her. He looked about the same, with a little more facial hair than she remembered, but it was him, undoubtedly. He stood silently, perhaps making his own study of the changes in her face. Tanya felt a mix of emotions surge through her as she sensed an involuntary reaction welling up in her throat.

'Hi, um—' she snapped.

'Cold hands?' he replied.

'No. I mean yes, but not anymore.' She rubbed her hands over the fire to illustrate.

'Hi. Uh … How've you been?' he asked, almost as an afterthought.

'Good, good. And you?'

'Yeah, me too,' he said with a hush. They both nervously stared at each other. 'Tanya, I'm so happy to see you.'

'Are you?'

'Of course I am. I missed you.'

'Then why haven't we spoken properly for over a year?' Tanya's voice felt like a needle slowly piercing its way through fabric. She couldn't recognise her own tone.

'I don't know … It just sort of happened.'

'You didn't even tell me you were in Delhi!'

'I am only here for two days for this wedding. I didn't think I would have the time to meet anyone.'

'It's okay. It was good seeing you, Aryan, and to know that you are doing well. I think I should go now. It's late too,' she blurted out, feeling a little out of breath.

'Please stay a little longer,' he pleaded.

'But why?'

'Just ... Honestly, I don't know how we stopped talking. But as time went by, I felt like there was this friction that developed between us. I just didn't know how to work past it. It was too strong.'

'But you knew you could always talk to me ...'

'I did, but I just became so confused after I went away. Everything suddenly felt too complicated.'

'I expected you to be around in spite of that,' she said softly, lowering her eyes.

'I'm sorry, I didn't mean to let you down.'

'It's alright. I think my expectations were too unrealistic. It's not that easy for people to be there for each other. And our lives did grow apart.'

'I'm sorry. I should've still been better.'

'No, don't feel bad. I'm just annoyed at my parents and I'm probably taking it out on you.'

'I heard that they separated. I'm so sorry. Do you want to talk about it?'

'No. Maybe later. Not right now.'

'Okay. Do you want to head out maybe, away from all this noise?'

'Alright, let's go,' Tanya sighed. They stepped outside, a dusty parking lot stretching before them. Only a few departing families disturbed the quiet. Aryan leaned against the back of a car and Tanya stood in front of him. A strong wind sent her open hair flying all over the place.

'Why don't you tie your hair up?'

'My clutch broke. It's just how some things are. Once they're broken, they can't be fixed,' she snapped. After a pause, she continued, 'Sorry, I sound spiteful.'

'No, you don't. Besides, there's always another way to mend what's broken,' he smiled, reaching for his wallet. He pulled out a black hair tie and motioned for Tanya to turn her head. Running his fingers through her hair, he succeeded in making a somewhat messy bun.

'Isn't this mine?' she asked with a subdued smile.

'Yes. The one you gave me when we last met.'

'Well, you're not half bad at this. Did you tie a lot of buns for all your girlfriends in London?'

'What do you mean? I didn't—'

'I got you,' Tanya started giggling.

'Hey, at least you're laughing now. It didn't seem like I would see that,' Aryan replied with a sense of relief.

'I was a lot more cheerful back in school, wasn't I? I don't know what's got into me. It's just been hard to laugh at anything recently.'

An abrupt pause came over the conversation and a knot of silence formed between them. Aryan desperately tried to untangle his way through it, but his mind drew a complete blank.

'Do you ever think that if someone's choices affect you, you should have a say in them?' Tanya asked all of a sudden.

'What do you mean?' Aryan was glad that the conversation was moving again.

'When my parents divorced, I had no say in any of it. I respect the decision they took for themselves, but it's still hard to accept it. I'm still stuck in the process of accepting it. It wasn't even my choice, but I have to live with it. Everyone seems to have forgotten that somehow.'

'You know, sometimes even if it is your choice, it doesn't matter. If you choose to do something, people expect you to be completely happy about it. Choices aren't perfect, but people like to pretend they are. Whenever I complain about something in London that seems out of place, everyone keeps reminding me that it was my decision to go.'

'I'm sorry about that. I guess we're all just victims of the choices we carry. Whether we made them or not is secondary.' Tanya leaned back next to Aryan, letting out a soft sigh that mingled with the cold evening air. 'God, that sounds so heavy and philosophical,' she chided herself.

'You know what I just realised?' he said as he looked her in the eye. 'We all get tangled with life's complexities, but life is actually quite simple. So simple, yet so fleeting. I don't know how long we would have taken to open up again if we hadn't met here. We should never have stopped talking. I'm really sorry.'

'I guess you're right. It was always quite simple for us to let each other know what we felt. We just put ourselves into these shells for some kind of protection. Maybe we were just scared.'

'Tanya, I don't want us to be like that anymore.'

'Do you want me to tell you how I feel? Completely unfiltered for once?' Tanya almost stuttered as she spoke.

'Yes,' he hummed in a low tone.

'Aryan, I think I really like you. Even now. I know that you—'

'I think I love you, Tanya,' he cut in. They froze for a while, then laughed nervously. Tanya smiled and nodded at him.

'So, um, what do we—what do we do about this?' she asked with a slight jitter in her jaw.

Aryan shrugged his shoulders, then wrapped his arms around her. Tanya leaned in and pressed her nose gently against his. They both started smiling and feeling a little out of breath. Then, in a simple and careful manner, they kissed, exchanging the coldness inside with a newly found warmth.

Aryan slammed his head against the tray table and forcefully closed his eyes. He had felt okay when the flight took off, but midway through the journey, he was sure that he would collapse. He felt as if someone had opened up a window within him and everything inside was fluttering around uncontrollably like loose pages trying to weather a heavy storm. The events of the wedding night played in a loop in his mind. Every attempt to fall asleep ended in frustration, leaving him helplessly awake.

As the pilot made their landing announcement, Aryan felt like something had dropped within him and he was finally able to cry. He couldn't tell if life had moved on ahead or if he had left it behind to enter something uncertain. All he knew was that no matter what, he would wait to be with Tanya again. Because he was helplessly in love. Love that wasn't singular. Love made up of so many fragments that he had to keep contained within himself. Maybe all it took was a black hair tie to hold all of them together. Only to be let loose for one person.

As the flight landed, Aryan wondered if it was him moving or the trees that were going backwards.

∼

Candy Says

'THERE ARE TOO MANY POTHOLES IN THIS CITY. I CAN'T WAIT to move,' a woman of about twenty-three said as she pulled a strand of hair away from her face. She looked beautiful in her black round-framed glasses.

'The place you're moving to has potholes too,' said the twenty-five-year-old man seated across her at a run-down cafe. He lifted his empty glass slightly and signalled to a waiter, silently requesting a refill.

'But it's so much more than that,' she grimaced at the plate in front of her, 'All the cafes here are dull and their food's so bland.'

'You used to love this cafe! You claimed that everything on the menu here was a delight to be discovered.'

'But there's a greater delight to be discovered away from here. If I stay here anymore, I'll lose my wits. I feel like I'm becoming an old woman. I need to move out, just to be myself again. This time it'll be perfect.'

'That's what you said the last four times. Yet here we are again. It's a pattern that keeps repeating itself.' He took a sip of his water and put the glass down a little too hard, spilling some of it.

'No one gets things right on their first try. Anyone who claims to is a liar trying to sabotage other people's lives.' She dabbed her mouth with a tissue and crumpled it into the palm of her hand.

'Haven't you had more than one attempt? How much longer do you intend to pursue this?'

'I promise it's the last time. I can tell.' They sat in silence for a while. She tapped her index finger on the table in varying rhythms, then stopped. 'Will you be following me again this time?' she winked at him.

'It was by pure chance that I found work in all of these cities you've dragged me to. The thing about chance, however, is that it runs out. You might have to be on your own this time. That's why you shouldn't go.' He clasped both hands tightly around his glass.

'I'll have to be on my own someday. I'll miss your company though.' She popped her lighter and lit up a cigarette. 'You know I've tried thirty-one different types now. I still don't know which one I prefer the most.'

'What about your boyfriend? How is he taking it?' He passed her the ashtray from a nearby table.

'We're through. He didn't want to deal with the distance. I'm happy it's over. He only ever wore blue shirts and listened to the same goddamn music over and over.'

'Think you'll still keep in touch with him?' he asked in a straight manner.

'I mean, we broke up.'

'You still talk to me though.'

'That's different. We're different. Oh, I almost forgot, I brought you a parting gift.' She produced a copy of *The Catcher in the Rye* by J.D. Salinger. 'I tried reading it but couldn't understand a damn thing that was happening. You're smart, so please read it for me. I've written my new address on the back. You'll write me a letter, won't you?'

He accepted the book and nodded in silence. They split the cheque and hugged as they parted. She was leaving by a bus late that night.

'Don't go, Ruhi,' his voice revealed a desperation that had managed to find a way out of his cold exterior.

'I wish I could stay, but the natural process of things will always take me away from anything that tries to become permanent. Nothing's permanent.' She let go of their embrace and mustered her best smile that formed a permanent imprint on his memory.

Maybe she was right in labelling the concept of permanence a lie of the highest order. I could've sworn I would never forget her smile on that day, yet all these years later I am struggling to remember.

Her family came from a long line of intellectual excellence, with generations achieving acclaim as poets, authors, musicians, lawyers and journalists. All of them had lived in the same city all their lives. While she carried her family's intellectual heirloom, her profession itself was a novelty. She was a teacher, starting out her career at twenty-one, right around the time I started dating her. She worked at the same school the last four generations of her family had attended, including her and her younger brother.

Agh, her brother! I met the little devil only a couple of times. He was the brightest kid of his age. Heck, he was smarter than people two years older. There was something about the way he used to speak that got on my nerves. It was as if he was always trying not to look down upon me out of sympathy. Bastard. He was, after all, destined to be the pinnacle of the family's years of achievement and he seemed to know that better than anyone else.

A peculiar thing about her family was that they were crazy about routines. They had the most bizarre ones aimed at 'maximising productivity', and they followed them better than anyone else could hope to. It was all quite intimidating but also incredibly intriguing. Every aspect of their day was precisely planned. However, it all fell apart one day when her brother went missing.

Song of the Day

He had been out cycling on his regular route, as he did every Tuesday. I remember the rain was really pouring down that evening, but he wasn't one to mess up his schedule for anything. He only knew one thoroughly calculated way of living life; anything else was unacceptable. A harsh resolve for someone who was only fourteen at the time.

When he failed to return home on time, his family informed the police that he had gone missing. The officer taking down their report must have been bemused by how sure they were about it. After all, a kid can always be late coming back home. But not him. He had disappeared without a trace. In the end, no one ever found him.

She met me a few days after his disappearance when, to my surprise, she was fifteen minutes late. We broke up that day. She quit her job too. Suddenly, she went from brilliance to being ordinary, but it seemed more like a conscious choice. Then came all the moving to different cities. I had no reason to follow her, yet I did. There was something beautiful about the idea of it that I could never resist. Each time, I tried to convince her and myself that it was only a coincidence, but she knew my bluff better than me. It was strange that my life should plot itself completely around her. Strange and somewhat bizarre. Even though I had told her at that cafe I wouldn't follow her again, I was always going to. But Ruhi never gave me that chance.

Later that evening after she parted with him, Ruhi went back to her apartment and lay in bed staring at the ceiling. The white plaster was peeling off because of the rain. After tossing her feet around for a while she finally shut her eyes. She felt glad that she wouldn't have to wake up to the same room anymore and her mind slipped into a slow sinking dream.

She was laid out on a wooden deck overlooking a flamingo-pink lake. The sun was in the middle of the sky, and it cast a spectacle of fragmented brilliance as it touched the water's surface. A swift breeze that smelled of cherries tangled with her hair. An excessive amount of stillness had seeped into the surroundings. In the distance, she spotted an object floating towards her. It was a pastel-yellow balloon with a lily tied at its end. The mysterious pair stopped exactly in front of her and hung there for a minute. Then the balloon popped, and the lily made a gentle splash as it fell into the lake. As she bent down to reach for it, something invisible pushed her into the water. Her body went limp; she slowly sank and drifted away with the currents. The water changed shades from pink to indigo to something that resembled milk. All the bubbles imploded as they released a blinding light. Everything turned white. Dazzlingly white. Dipped in the absence of gravity. No end in sight. And then she woke up, flat on her bed, to the complete darkness of her room.

It was around 8 p.m. and the doorbell was ringing a soft chime. Her mouth was dry, and her hair looked fuzzy. She had a long, stained T-shirt on that covered her shorts completely. On

Song of the Day

maybe the fifth ring of the bell she opened the main gate, but there was no one outside. She waited expectantly at the door for a minute, and a boy of about ten sprung out of nowhere.

'Boo!' he screamed.

'Oh my God!' she replied, pretending to be scared. The little boy lived next door. He often came over to play with her.

'Play cards with me?' he asked as he pulled his T-shirt down and swayed his body, an expectant smile on his face.

'Sure. Come on in. Playing games with you is just what I need to make my day.' She didn't have much choice. He was one of those stubborn kids who wouldn't take a no for an answer.

'Before we start, can I get a chocolate?'

'I'm all out of chocolates today, sorry,' she shrugged. He puffed his face into a frown and sat on the floor with his arms crossed.

'Fine, let's just play go fish,' he said.

'You got it, chief.'

She dealt the cards, and they played a few games. He won all of them and kept teasing her about it. He was the kind of kid who couldn't take a loss well, so she kept letting him win. After seven straight losses though, she got bored of his incessant trash talk and decided to play for real. He lost the eighth game. It made his temper flare, and he threw all the cards away in disgust. She couldn't contain herself and burst out laughing.

'You're mean!' he shrieked as he broke into tears and hit her across the face. She grabbed hold of both his hands with force and glared at him. It was enough for the boy to realise that it would be in his best interest to shut up. Her angry stare mellowed into a smile once he was quiet.

'I won't talk to you anymore,' he sobbed.

'That will make me sad. What can I do to make it up to you?' she replied.

'I don't know, let me think.' He pondered about it for a minute, then got all excited. 'Oh, I know! Can I water your plants?'

'Water my plants? I already—' she said but suddenly broke off. She realised she had forgotten to water her plants. 'It's cold tonight, isn't it? I already watered my plants in the morning. Maybe I can do something else for you. Do you want a chocolate?'

'Liar! You said you didn't have chocolates!'

'Do you want one or not?'

'Yes please,' he smiled, a little embarrassed. She let go of him and walked up to the fridge, emerging with three chocolates moments later. He jumped with joy.

'Go home and eat dinner, then have these. Don't forget to brush your teeth after that, okay?' she instructed him. He nodded. She handed the chocolates over and knelt down to give him a tight hug.

'You're weird,' he said. She kissed him on the cheek and let him go. He happily raced off back to his house and the door slammed shut after him. 'This is it. It's the last time I'll see that little boy. Seeing him was becoming a routine,' she thought to herself as she bit her lip. 'He will soon become another person to be looked at only through the window of the past.'

Thinking of a window, her mind shifted to her plants, and she went to the balcony to check on them. They hadn't been watered on time. It felt strange because she had never forgotten about them. The first thing she did every morning was take care of them. It was an unspoken rule. It wasn't meant to be broken. The thought of her mistake made her laugh. Seized by a whim, she plucked all the flowers and laid them out neatly over the kitchen counter. They seemed to smile at her, and she smiled back. She then waved goodbye to them and left the kitchen.

Back in her room, she switched on a red night lamp. Everything casually flirted with its dull glow. She put on a few Beatles songs on repeat and danced as she smoked three whole packs of Marlboros. They left a bitter dryness in her mouth, and the smoke made her lightheaded. It felt strangely refreshing. As if the room had opened up and the walls had fallen apart.

Once she was exhausted, she crashed onto her bed and listened to *Candy Says* by The Velvet Underground. She used a finger to make beautiful patterns in the air. As the song ended, her eyes started to droop. By then it was 11 p.m. 'Time to go,' she reasoned; her bus was to arrive in two hours. All her stuff was packed up. But for the life of her she couldn't remember where she was going. She had also forgotten to eat anything and to water her plants.

Candy Says

She went to the balcony to check on the plants, but none of them had flowers anymore. They had all been cut off. She followed their scent to the kitchen and chopped some vegetables for dinner, then slit her wrists and gently passed away.

Gulaabi

'Excuse me, ma'am, can I please borrow one of your earrings,' a twenty-three-year-old man asked a woman of about the same age as they stood outside the exit gates of Mumbai's international airport. 'I know it sounds strange, but I need to change the SIM on my phone. I don't have a pin or any other way to take out the tray.'

'Sure,' she replied as she carefully removed one of her minarets and handed it to the man. He smiled at her and took a couple of minutes going through the motions of opening and closing his phone before returning the earring.

'I'm sorry, I think we've met before,' she said as she held on to the small gold object. 'Aren't you Jahan? We went to college in Pune together. I'm Kavya. I don't know if you remember—'

'Kavya! I'm sorry I didn't recognise you. Wow! How are you?'

'I'm … good. And you?'

'Thereabouts. I just got back from Dubai. I was there on a work assignment for two days. Here, this is me now,' he said as he reached into his wallet and handed her a business card that read 'Sales Associate'.

'Dubai sounds wonderful,' Kavya said as she put the card away in her clutch.

'Yeah, it's okay,' he replied, and they looked at each other uncertainly. The air grew still with unspoken words, until the distant whir of planes in the sky took over.

'So, where are you headed?' Kavya asked, breaking the silence as she stuffed her hands deep into her pockets.

'King's Circle. I live pretty close to it.'

'Hey, I'm headed to that area too. Would you like to come with me?'

'If that's okay with you,' Jahan smiled as he let his bag slide on to one shoulder.

The two of them walked to the taxi zone and boarded a cab after waiting for a few minutes. Soon, rusted light poles and worn reflectors moved past them at a steady pace. It was an early Saturday morning outside and the moon still peeked down at people from a cloudy veil. Black birds flew around in the distance in happy groups of three or four.

Song of the Day

'You're a light traveller,' Kavya said as she carefully buckled her seatbelt in. The air conditioner blew cold air against her calves.

'Yeah, I didn't want to carry more than a backpack for just a two-day visit,' Jahan replied. His head was rested against the tinted car window.

'You know I wouldn't blame you for not recognising me. We were in different departments.'

'You were in Fine Arts, and I was in Commerce. I don't know if that's a world apart.'

'So, you actually do remember me,' Kavya said as she turned away from Jahan with a smile.

'Of course, why would I lie?' He sat up straight at once.

'I'm sorry, it's just—you would always bunk college, so I thought there was no way you would recognise me.'

'I see where you're coming from,' he laughed. 'It was convenient. Everyone knew I played football. So, once in a while I would come to college with a crepe bandage on and pretend to have had an injury. The professors were kind enough to let my attendance slide.'

'That's pretty creative.'

'I guess so. But that's not the real reason I missed classes so often. I—' he paused abruptly, before continuing, 'I used to work part-time at a call centre to support my family through most of college.' Jahan opened a bottle of water and drank a small amount from it, his eyes stuck tracing depressions in the car roof.

'Oh … I didn't—know that.'

'No one did. I was pretty embarrassed about it to tell anyone. My dad's grocery shop wasn't doing well. My younger sister was still in school,' he continued as he managed to look directly at her.

'I think it's remarkable to do that at such a young age.' Kavya ran her fingers through her hair and gently straightened a few strands out. They had halted at a traffic signal, and a young boy was walking around selling roses outside. He smiled at Jahan and Kavya as he passed by their window.

'For the longest time I was just bitter about it. The fact that almost everyone else around me got to be a normal student while I had to work.'

'And now?' she asked.

Jahan smiled at Kavya. 'I used to save some money every month and put it away. Over three years, I had accumulated a large enough amount. My sister turned eighteen the year we graduated. I was able to pay for her college.' Passenger buses drifted by on the other side as he spoke and people made their way towards railway station platforms in unbroken heaps.

'When you handed me that visiting card and said "This is me now", it felt so weird. Like we're at that age now where it's a normal thing to do. Kind of strange, right?'

'Yeah, a bit, I would say,' Jahan admitted after some thought.

Kavya rested her palms against the velvet taxi seat and its warmth reminded her of the feeling of being held close. 'You know, I pretended for some time at the airport,' she spoke softly.

Song of the Day

'What do you mean?' he asked in a warm voice.

'I recognised you instantly. I just waited because I was nervous.'

~

'Do you want to get breakfast?' Jahan asked once they had settled the cab fare. Kavya agreed, and they decided to go to an old cafe by King's Circle. A bowl of Maggi and an omelette was ordered to be shared along with a cup of chai each.

'I love this place. They shot *The Lunchbox* here,' Kavya said as she leaned back into a worn wooden chair, its once-sharp edges softened by the passage of time. 'I wish someone would write a book about love and cinema in Bombay.'

'You're very fond of films, aren't you?'

'They have a magic to them.'

'Kavya, are you seeing someone?' Jahan blurted out abruptly.

'No ... It's been a while,' she pressed her lips together. 'Are you?'

'Not really, no. I've had a hard time finding that special connection with someone,' he replied as he wrapped his hands around the warm cup of chai. 'But I'm sure it'll happen,' he added after a moment.

'Are you still in touch with anyone from college?'

'Most people moved pretty far away, didn't they?' They smiled at each other. A waiter brought their order to the table, quickly placing everything down.

'By the way, I'm bad at sharing food, so you'll have to keep up,' Kavya stared at Jahan with a serious expression.

'If that's the case, then I challenge you to a sword fight!' he exclaimed as he pulled the bowl of Maggi towards his side and started blocking Kavya's fork with his own. They fought for a while and almost spilled the food onto the table several times. Eventually, they ended up laughing at each other uncontrollably.

'Oh my God! Fine! I'll share,' Kavya smirked and shook her head.

'What kind of work do you do now?' Jahan asked as he shifted the bowl back to the centre of the table.

'I assist an art collector during the week and sometimes paint on the weekends in my downtime.'

'I've never been a creative person. What kind of subjects inspire you?'

'All sorts of things. People on the street. Failed romances. Footballers stuck making sales pitches.'

'That's funny,' Jahan laughed.

'My goal used to be becoming an artist full-time, but I think I want to work on highlighting other artists now. Supporting their stories. Do you know what you're looking for from your job?'

'I want to be financially independent and stable enough to adopt a kid.'

'Wow! That's really kind. Why specifically, if I may ask?'

'I feel like I've lived an entire life without ever being anyone's first priority. My parents always had their focus on raising my older brother. I realised over time that I want to care for someone and make them my first priority. And maybe giving is the only way of ever receiving that affection.'

'You're so sure of what you want,' Kavya said in an almost proud manner.

'Aren't you?' Jahan asked.

'I feel, in some ways, I'm still finding my feet here. Like, I know what trains to take and what food to cook and maybe even how to manage my money, but it's just something about living life that I'm still discovering … If that makes sense.'

'It does …' he replied as he stared at her affectionately.

Kavya and Jahan talked for some more time and split the cheque afterward. As they exited the cafe, they walked on in silence for a while in no clear direction.

'I want to read a book. Do you have any recommendations?' Kavya asked as they stopped by a row of booksellers on the street. Jahan scanned the stalls for a few minutes before picking up a copy of *The Little Prince*. His fingers grazed softly against its narrow spine as he handed it to Kavya.

'Why this one?' she asked as she paid for the book.

'It calmed me and opened my heart when I read it.'

'I'm sure I'll find something in it to keep with me too then,' Kavya said as she hugged the paperback close to her chest. 'So, as I was saying, this idea of being in large friend groups, I'm not good at that kind of thing,' she continued, picking up a conversation they'd left incomplete. 'But maybe that'll change one day and—'

'Kavya, can I walk you home?' Jahan asked all of a sudden. 'I want to continue having these conversations with you.'

'Sure,' Kavya nodded with a smile. 'Thank you. It's … been a while since anyone has really talked to me,' she went on.

'I've enjoyed this too,' he replied.

'Do you like it here?' she asked after some time. 'Being in Mumbai?'

'I was frustrated by it for a while. By the rush the city carried and the energy it demanded from me. But then, one day I was going to the airport when the traffic was terrible, and I realised it was almost like the city was trying to cling on to me like a person who'd fallen in love—asking me not to leave that day. To stay … just for a while. I fell in love with Bombay in that single moment.'

As Jahan finished speaking, Kavya tugged at his sleeve without much of a thought and held him gently for a moment. Jahan shyly placed his arms inwards as they eventually broke their embrace. They walked on in stillness and passed through a narrow lane whose walls hugged the city warm.

'I pause here sometimes,' Kavya said to Jahan as they stopped at the centre of the lane and stood idly. 'I'm always by myself when I'm here, yet today I finally feel calm. It's funny, I'm sure we had such different upbringings and yet somehow—you have the fragrance of being home,' her gaze searched his eyes as she spoke.

'Is it okay if I hold your hand?' Jahan asked quietly as he slowly outstretched his arm.

Song of the Day

'I want to know more about you,' Kavya said as she gently placed her hand in his.

'How should we do that?'

'Play me a song that you like,' she replied. He put some thought into it, then played a track called *Gulaabi* by Ishaan Kaushik on his phone.

'Jahan,' Kavya said as she placed her head on his shoulder, 'we still have our entire lives ahead of us, don't we?' They looked at each other with their heads tilted and smiled widely for a long time.

Iktara

'People often try to console children by saying the dead become stars. Why didn't anyone ever do that with me?' Rishi asked as he folded a used tissue in a criss-cross pattern.

'Maybe they just couldn't lie to you,' Nithya replied.

'Liar,' Rishi smirked as they walked about a park blooming a New York summer. People in wooden gondolas rowed through small, pale water lakes. Kids lay on their stomachs here and there with their elbows planted in the sunburnt grass.

'Why do you always fold your trash like that before throwing it away?' Nithya asked.

'A girl I once knew told me about it. People in Korea fold their trash this way so that it takes up less space.'

'That kind of girl?' Nithya smiled.

'No, not that kind of girl,' Rishi protested, dipping his hands into his cardigan pockets. Broken leaves flew through the air, embracing people at times.

'You're lucky you're a guy. My parents just want me to find someone and get married.' Nithya let herself fall onto the grass and Rishi lay down next to her. He watched her face as she looked through the sky.

'We're twenty-five now. You don't need anyone's instructions.'

'Yeah, I was just joking,' she punched him meekly in the shoulder.

'Of course, I'm sorry,' he said quietly. 'So, no one, huh?'

'There is this guy. But he moved to New York a long time ago and I still live in Mumbai,' she giggled to herself.

'Nithya, you just want to trouble me.' He turned onto his back and closed his eyes.

'Do you think we would've dated if you hadn't moved?' She curled towards him as she spoke.

'What's the point of thinking about that?' He put an arm around her and slowly stroked her head. 'There's no way I wouldn't have moved.'

They crossed out onto an avenue clothed in the morning sun. A woman cleaning tall cafe windows greeted them in passing as people darted in and out of subway entrances in a constant rush.

'What's your brother doing now?' Rishi asked.

'He works at a consulting firm. I think he wants to continue that for another year and then get a master's. Maybe here or in the UK.'

'Seems like a lot of people have been moving recently. Would you consider it?'

'If my brother leaves, then I'll definitely stay back to be close to my parents.' Nithya walked with her hands crossed behind her back. A glass pendant shaped like Saturn's rings hung around her neck. 'Although this weather could tempt me,' she added as an afterthought.

'The winters can be harsh, but then spring and summer come along, and New York is a city healed anew.' The wind blew strongly, kissing their hair frantically like an excited child and they watched each other and laughed.

'Seems like the city liked what you said,' Nithya said as they stopped by Rishi's apartment building. She dipped her hand in a fountain built at its entrance and flicked a fistful of water at Rishi's face with a giggle. He laughed with a shake of his head. The doorman pulled open a beautiful wooden door and tipped his cap towards them. They climbed up a silent stairway inside and walked through a passage covered with windows on either side. Nithya waited on Rishi to unlock the apartment door as the sound of him fumbling with the keys formed a wind chime's rustle.

'Do you remember that magic trick you used to do as a kid?' Nithya asked as she stood at the centre of the doorway with her head tilted to one side. An old metal clock with a Victoria terminus dial filled the silence of the living room wall.

'The one with paper?'

'Yes! What did you call it?'

'Tokyo Star,' Rishi replied as they sat down next to each other. 'I was bad at craft and my classmates would make fun of me, so my teacher taught me a trick that she had learnt when visiting Tokyo. It was a way of folding a piece of paper and tearing out the outline of a circle from it. And yet the magic was that when the torn-out part would be opened, it would appear in the shape of a star. No one else in the class could do what I could after that.'

'No one else can do what you can,' Nithya said with a playful nudge. 'I've realised New York is a lot like Mumbai,' she continued as she glanced outside a window covered in water stains.

'Maybe that's why I'm here.'

'My flight seems to be on time, I should leave soon,' she said as she checked her phone and tossed it aside with a hush.

'You know, I wish I could make you stay for longer,' Rishi ran his hands through Nithya's hair lovingly as he spoke. 'That this could be everyday life—picking up the mail, shopping at grocery stores, assembling furniture with you.'

'Why not come back to Mumbai then?' She held him with one arm around his neck.

'You know why, Nitya,' he started as he let his weight fall on her. 'I used to stare at the sky every night back then. The stars never changed their alignment. It was always the same. The dead remain the dead.'

'Nakul and Shaan always ask me about you,' Nithya said after some time.

'How are they?'

'You should call them to know,' she tried to smile at him.

'You know, it's hard …'

'We miss you … I miss you. Maybe if you moved back, we could—' Nithya broke off as her eyes met Rishi's.

'You know I can't return to that place anymore. Please stop asking me about it.'

'Why? You asked me if I would move here.'

'That's different, you know that. You're just hurting me,' he said, lowering his gaze to Nithya's feet.

'I have a flight to catch, and you have work to get to,' she said after some thought.

'But there's still time. I'm sorry, I didn't mean that.'

'I know, come here,' Nithya held Rishi close again as she spoke and patted his head gently before letting him go. 'I'll go get my stuff. Can you call me a cab?' she asked, and Rishi nodded.

A few minutes later, they were downstairs and had loaded Nithya's luggage into the cab. The morning bloom of the city had grown distant, and they hugged each other silently in a longing manner. Nithya's shoes rubbed against the gravel as she eventually walked away from Rishi.

Song of the Day

Once the cab drove away, Rishi didn't feel like going back up to his apartment. He walked outside for a while before entering a cafe that he was fond of. Glass baskets filled with sugar packets were carefully placed on each table inside. He sat there drinking an iced coffee for a while until all of the ice had melted completely. A little boy sitting at the table next to him was lying down with his head placed sideways. Rishi laid his head down to face the boy. After some time, the little boy waved towards Rishi, and he waved back. The boy quickly got up and rolled a newspaper his father had been reading into a cylinder.

'Look at me through the tunnel,' he said with an excited urgency as he laid back down again. Rishi moved close to him and looked through the hole with a smile.

'I can see you,' the boy giggled. 'What do you see?'

'I ... see you too,' Rishi replied as he watched the little boy's eye. It reminded him of peeking through a keyhole, patiently waiting for someone to return home. He waved goodbye to the boy and walked out onto the street. A cool breeze held him in its embrace. He walked a couple of blocks with the leaves flying alongside him before stopping to call Nithya.

'Hi—' he cried as he spoke.

'Rishi ...' she replied softly and waited for him to speak.

'Nithya ... there are so many things I feel sometimes that I try to say, but I always cannot until the last moment. And then everything is rushed,' he continued crying.

'Tell me now.'

'I don't want to regret this. I don't want to spend my time thinking one way about life, only to realise one day that I was wrong. That life was meant to be something else altogether.'

'Even if we're wrong, I'm with you; until the end.' Nithya's voice held a slice of warmth.

'You know I love you. I always will. No matter how far we are.'

'I do, we all do. I know you think there's not much to come back to in Mumbai, but we will love you forever, Rishi. We will always be home for you.'

'I'll come home soon,' Rishi sniffled and smiled as he spoke. The first drops of rain had started to appear around New York by then.

***

Rishi came home. Many times. And yet, the visits grew shorter each time and further apart. I woke up one day to realise that he had spent more of his life away from Mumbai than in Mumbai. A harsh sense of grief gripped me at the realisation. Maybe it was because I knew he would never move back now. But I also felt happy for the life he had carved out for himself. And the courage he had carried in his heart.

Many years ago, a night in November changed everything about a boy that we were all fond of. Rishi had rung the doorbell to our place and declared that he was tired of waiting for his parents to return home. We ended up keeping him at our house all night as pellets of lead were being scattered across Mumbai. Two days and nights passed by, achingly slow. The third morning, his uncle came, swollen eyed, to pick him up from our house. After that day, I realised that friends must also become family sometimes.

Once Rishi turned sixteen, his uncle accepted a transfer to the States. We were all there to see him off at the airport when he flew to New York for the first time; perhaps naively unaware of how far apart our lives were about to lead us. I remember the first time I had seen him cry. We had gone to the cinema to watch *Wake Up Sid*. When the song *Iktara* played, he just started to weep inconsolably. We spent many following months waiting for the song to play on the radio, and sometime after that, I gifted him a CD containing the movie's album. That day when I left New York ended up being the last time he ever cried to me.

On Rishi's thirty-sixth birthday, I spoke to him briefly and he told me that he was getting married. Once I kept the phone down, I couldn't help but cry. I realised my memories of Rishi, like an old paper star, had faded and crumpled and disintegrated into bits. Yet, every year, I had held them fondly against my chest, searching frantically for a smell that had grown on me with time. My eyes trying to follow footprints in the mud from many monsoons gone by. Hoping to find a Tokyo Star moving away from me.

Blackbird

Sakshi smiled at Raghav as she emptied two packets of half and half into her abnormally strong coffee. It was raining outside, and the sound of the steady downpour overlapped with the chatter of voices around them in the coffee shop. *Blackbird* by The Beatles played tenderly in the background. Sakshi couldn't place a finger on it, but for some reason, she loved the first five spoonsful of her coffee and absolutely hated the rest. On tasting the sixth spoon, she passed the remainder of it to Raghav who shakily picked it up and almost spilt the cup. He drew a slow breath in.

'This seems wrong. Are you sure about this?' he asked her.

Sakshi stared at his hands, then clasped them at once and nodded. 'It's alright,' she said, her grip gentle over his wrists, gaze aligned with his eyeline. Raghav nodded back with a lingering uncertainty. She planted a kiss on each of his hands and lifted them to her cheeks.

'That's left lipstick stains,' he said with the first traces of a genuine smile.

'They're happy stains though, aren't they?' Raghav nodded back repeatedly with glee. She joined in and both of them started nodding vigorously as they tried to contain their laughter.

'Let's do this then. Shall we?' Raghav asked in a whisper.

'Yes please. Besides, the coffee's dreadful,' Sakshi smirked. She picked up her bag, Raghav gathered his bearings, and on a whim, they dashed out of the cafe without sparing a second thought for the bill. A group of waiters shouted at them to stop and a few even made chase, but they were soon out of sight as they disappeared into the rain mist outside.

They slowed down once they had put a safe distance between themselves and the chasing mob of waiters. Raghav held tightly on to Sakshi's hand, squeezing it affectionately, and they gently walked on as they caught their breath in between silly laughs and occasional sneezes. The downpour had completely soaked their clothes by then and a dark wash of grey hung over the sky. As they reached back to Raghav's car a few minutes later, Sakshi pulled him to the side, stood on her toes, and kissed him with all her heart.

~

Six months later

'Do we really need to go?' Raghav asked as he stared at himself in the mirror and rolled down the sleeves of his shirt. He thought it was better that way.

'Everyone we know is going,' Maya replied as she put an arm around Raghav's chest. Her black nail polish shone under the light fixture above their dresser. She placed a warm kiss on the back of his neck.

'Fine,' Raghav said as he shakily turned her arm away.

They gathered the last bits of their belongings and headed down to the parking lot. Maya's heels knocked harshly against the grey concrete floor as she walked. A winter hush slipped in from the air outside. Raghav unlocked their car and sat down in the driver's seat. Maya's reflection formed in the rear-view mirror. He turned it away.

As Raghav drove, scores of traffic signs passed by. Maya and he hardly made any conversation. Small specks of stars shone softly in an otherwise clouded sky. Flyovers remained lively but quiet. They halted at a red light and a kid in old misfitting clothes approached their car asking for something to eat. Raghav lowered his window and gave the little boy a hundred-rupee note. He smiled and blew a kiss towards Raghav before running away with a hop in his step.

'You know they're giving all that money away to their alcoholic masters,' Maya said in a grainy voice. She pressed her fingers against her temples.

'Maybe, but I still have hope.'

'Whatever suits you.'

'I'm going to leave the window lowered,' Raghav continued. 'I want to feel the air on my face.'

They drove on and after some time, Raghav and Maya walked into an upscale hotel ballroom, arm in arm. Someone in their social circle had decided to hold a gathering for their first wedding anniversary. They greeted the couple and went around meeting various people who had shown up in their perfected outfits, prepared to talk and drink the night away. It was the usual chatter that flitted across the room. Whose kids were drug addicts and who was in trouble with the tax department. Discussions about politics and the stock market, and who had bought the most exquisite jewellery pieces.

'Raghav! How are you?' an old man called out in a jolly voice.

'Mr Agarwal, it's good to see you. Is Mrs Agarwal here too?' Raghav asked. He had been trotting around alone since a group of Maya's friends had drawn her away from him a while ago.

'Just me and Rohit,' Mr Agarwal replied. 'Look, there he is. Come here, son!' A young man aimlessly passing by walked over to where they were standing.

'Hello, father. Hello, Raghav,' Rohit said cheerfully.

'Raghav, I want to you to talk to this son of mine and guide him.'

'What can I guide him about? We're practically the same age,' Raghav replied.

'But look at you, you're so well settled. I heard from your father you're being tipped to become the youngest partner at your law firm. And you got married, what, almost two years ago now? Rohit is hardly serious about work or women. Those are the two most important things for a man. Even Maya has been taking her father's business forward. It is quite commendable. But my son here won't even step into my office,' Mr Agarwal shook his head for effect.

'Construction's dead, father,' Rohit cut in as he grabbed two drinks from a waiter and passed one of them to Raghav before downing the other.

'Construction can never be dead. It can only fall asleep. That's the foundation of Indian society. Only people who've seen the real world like Raghav and I can perceive such a hidden truism. Isn't that right, Raghav?'

'You flatter me is all I can say,' Raghav replied. Rohit leaned inwards all of a sudden and sniffed Raghav's collar. His warm breath hung over Raghav's neck until he drew himself back a few seconds later.

'I'm sorry. I was just trying to smell out your flaws,' Rohit smiled. Mr Agarwal glared at him, but when Raghav started laughing, his gaze lost its intensity at once.

'Forgive my boy. He has an old habit of joking around. He gets it from his mother.'

'Come on, father, humour is important too,' Rohit replied.

'I agree. Humour is all important.' Raghav took another sip of his drink with a smile.

'You can have your humour, Rohit. But please don't try to steal my husband,' Maya cut in as she appeared at Raghav's side and wrapped her hands around his arm.

'Who could blame me if I tried?' Rohit smirked.

'You look beautiful as always, my child,' Mr Agarwal chimed in.

'You look sharp too, Mr Agarwal. You seem to have lost some weight. Have you been working out?'

'Nothing of the sort! Just drinking the right kind of tea. I had sent the recipe to your father too. How is he doing?'

'He's doing well. Though I believe he has been missing your company.'

'He's been the one too busy to spare time for an old friend,' Mr Agarwal laughed to himself. 'Give him my regards, will you?'

'Certainly.'

'I'll take your leave now. Unless any of you care to join me in the smoking room? Raghav?'

'Oh no, thank you, sir.'

'That's good. It's a bad habit to keep anyway. Though I'll die if I quit now,' he hooted to himself, and the others supportively laughed.

'Maya, my father mentioned you were into some sort of social work,' Rohit said once Mr Agarwal had walked away from their circle.

'Did he now? Yes, it's something I'm very passionate about. I think it's important to help the poor. Especially kids. I've been meaning to make a donation to a children's home through our firm. Just need to find the right one. The people running these things are all so corrupt.'

'I cannot agree more with that. You know, I know a few people at this party who might have the right contacts. Shall I introduce you to them?'

'That would be lovely,' she smiled.

'Let's go right now? Can you grab me another glass of wine, Raghav?'

'Sure,' he replied as he reached for a tray of glasses on a small table and shakily picked one up, almost spilling it as he handed it to Rohit.

'Your hands tend to wander, don't they?' Rohit smiled.

'I'm sorry?'

'Nothing really. I have a habit of mumbling to myself. Anyway, enjoy the party.' He raised his glass to Raghav who returned the gesture. Maya and Rohit walked away into the crowd after that, chatting away. Once they had left, Raghav carefully made his way outside the ballroom and walked to the end of a long corridor at the other side of the hotel.

'You're late,' Sakshi said as she tilted her head and smiled at Raghav.

'I know, I'm sorry,' he replied and gave her a Ferrero Rocher from his pocket.

'Raghav,' she laughed as she took the chocolate from his palm. 'Are you sure we can talk here?'

'No one's going to come this way.'

Song of the Day

'Come here then,' Sakshi said as she drew Raghav close and kissed his forehead. He stood still with his eyes shut for a moment and twirled his little finger around hers.

'I'm sorry. This is my fault.' Raghav slipped back two steps to the fringe of Sakshi's grip.

'Never say that,' her fingers grazed against his cheek as she spoke. She clutched on to a few loose clumps of his hair. 'But you need to end this soon, Raghav. I've loved the first five months that we've been together, but I've absolutely hated the rest. It's dreadful, seeing the way things are.'

'I feel like I'm stuck in this position. Anytime I try to make up my mind I get scared of what will happen. But you restore my faith.' Raghav drew his hands level with Sakshi's waist as he spoke. She leaned in, almost kissing his lips.

'Then we need to try—'

'Maybe Raghav went this way. My my, what do we have here!' Rohit exclaimed as he appeared around the corner with Maya at his side. 'That's a kind way to treat a woman, isn't it?'

'Sure, must feel good,' Maya said as she turned around and stormed away from the corridor in an instant.

'I'm sorry, Sakshi,' Raghav said as he let go of her slowly. She tried to hold on to his hands, but they slipped out of her gentle grip.

'Please, don't—' she managed to say but Raghav had already run away to go after Maya. She closed her fist tightly around the gradually melting chocolate.

Back inside the ballroom Raghav looked all around for Maya but failed to place her anywhere in the crowd. 'Did Maya leave? Oh, that's a shame,' Rohit said as he followed Raghav about sheepishly.

'Cut it out, will you?' Raghav snapped.

'You know, just between the two of us, I don't know why you'd fancy that other woman over Maya. She had me aroused the entire evening.'

'You're just shallow and vain. Never thought you'd amount to much.'

'Those are big words coming from an adulterer,' Rohit smirked.

'Yeah? Why don't I stop talking and break your face then?'

'Oh, but you wouldn't do that. Too many people around who know you. Anyway, have a good night. I know I've had a wonderful one.' Rohit smiled as he bowed and left in the direction of the bar. Raghav stood alone at the centre of the ballroom helplessly looking for Maya in every face he saw.

After a while, Raghav abandoned his search and drove back home alone amidst the harsh noise of the car engine. He entered the apartment to the sound of music playing from the bathroom. The door was left ajar, and he walked in to find Maya in the bathtub smoking a cigarette with a wine glass placed beside her.

'Maya, I—' he started.

'If you planned on getting a divorce, I'm sure you would have done it by now,' she said, cutting him off. Raghav heaved a sigh and nodded without meeting her eyes. 'You'll be good now, won't you?' Her voice seemed to be cracking up. She took another puff of her cigarette.

'Yes, I will. I'm sorry.'

'Pour me some wine, won't you, love? I need to drink this off.' She held up her empty glass. Raghav obeyed and carefully poured out another serving from the bottle that lay on the cold lifeless floor. He placed the glass back in her hand, still evading her gaze. She took a sip of the wine before letting it rest behind her on the base of the bathtub.

'Come here, love,' she said as she tugged at the cuff of his shirt, and he let himself be led towards her. 'You're so fucking embarrassing, you know,' she whispered harshly as she rolled up Raghav's sleeve. He closed his eyes, and she pressed the tip of her cigarette against his wrist.

'It hurts. I'm sorry.' A tear slipped from his face onto the tiling underneath and her grip tightened around his hand. 'I'm sorry,' he repeated as the cigarette slipped further up and seemed to grow warmer. The abandoned glass of wine breathed in the backdrop as ash accumulated loosely around it.

~

The next morning Maya awoke to the sound of birds chirping on the bedroom windowsill. She slammed her hand against the glass panelling and the group flew away into the sunlit sky, possibly never to return. A little while later, Raghav woke up on the living room couch and got ready for work in a rush. As he dressed up to leave, he stared at himself in the mirror and rolled down the sleeves of his shirt. He thought it was better that way.

~

Thirteen

Ages: 8, 9

'D-I-C-T-I-O-N-A-R-Y. Dictionary,' an eight-year-old girl read out loud from the cover of a deep blue *Oxford English Dictionary*. She lovingly held the book against her chest.

'What does that mean?' the nine-year-old boy standing opposite her in the white and maroon tiled school corridor asked. His crisply ironed white shirt was carefully tucked into his dark-brown shorts. A moist monsoon air permeated the space between them.

'It's a book that tells you what other words mean. My father gifted it to me.'

'Wow. It looks so heavy. What will you do with it?'

Thirteen

'Learn a new word. Every day,' she replied excitedly.

'If you don't use it, give it to me. I'll use it to squash mosquitoes,' he said as he swung his hands in an illustrative manner.

'Shut up!' She drew herself away from him as he started laughing. A teacher rang the school bell thrice just then to mark the end of the lunch break, and scores of screaming kids with neatly combed hair started running back to the classrooms in their polished white canvas shoes.

'Wait for me after school,' she said with one step turned away from him.

'I will. Bye, Aanya,' he said with a smile.

'Bye, Dhruv,' she happily replied.

～

Ages: 9, 9

'Come home today. I got you a gift,' Aanya said to Dhruv as they got off their yellow school bus filled to the brim with children donning colourful raincoats and small lunch bags hanging by their sides. The two of them had lived in opposite buildings since they were three.

'What is it?' Dhruv asked as he held a deep-blue umbrella over their heads. Red tail lights floated through the rain drops as the bus drove away with a gentle swerve and left behind mud trails.

'I went with my mother to the market and got two fishbowls. One for me and one for you,' she replied as she stretched out her hand to collect some rain drops. A half-full purple water bottle hung around her neck.

'What are we supposed to do with them if we don't have any fishes? You're funny,' Dhruv giggled to himself. The sound of their feet splashing about in the water wrapped itself around the edges of his voice.

'We can share my dictionary and learn new words together. Then we can write down the ones we like the most on chits and store them in our bowls.'

'Hmm,' he considered it for a moment. 'I don't think I like learning words that much,' he eventually concluded in a disheartened voice.

'Oh,' she mumbled with a glum expression.

'Wait, I have an idea!' he suddenly started again. 'My older brother gave me his Walkman before going to college so that I could listen to music. I can write down the names of my favourite songs.' A strong gust tried to take their umbrella along with it, making his hands unsteady for a moment.

'Yes! I like that,' she smiled at him.

'I'm very smart, see!' he proudly replied.

'I'm smarter than you,' she retorted.

'No, you're not! I'll prove it to you,' he retaliated, but Aanya simply crossed her hands, closed her eyes and shook her head. Dhruv pulled the umbrella away from her in response, leaving her to get drenched in the rain. She quickly ran back towards him and slapped his shoulder as some water dripped from her face.

'I'm sorry,' he laughed loudly. She took hold of the umbrella and pushed him outside. He slowly walked back in, and they both began laughing.

'By the way, which word did you learn today?' Dhruv asked as they stood under Aanya's building.

'T-o-k-e-n. Token. It means something that is the symbol of a feeling,' she replied as she pressed a button to call for the elevator.

'I like that word. Token.'

'Maybe I can put it in my bowl.'

'We'll do it together when I come in the evening, okay?' he said as she waved goodbye to him and disappeared into the elevator. The rain had intensified by then. Dhruv closed his umbrella with a big smile and walked back home completely soaked.

∽

Ages 12, 13

Aanya and Dhruv had cycled through several semesters and finally reached the eighth grade. It meant that the boys' uniform had changed from shorts to full pants. Notebooks had been done away with in favour of loose sheet pads and multicoloured subject organisers. The all-encompassing field of General Science had been broken up into Physics, Chemistry and Biology, each with its separate textbook. Dhruv had started playing basketball for the school team that year and would attend practice every day in the morning before classes began. As a result, he had stopped going to school with Aanya in the mornings, and she would often sit by herself on the bus, watching traffic accumulate outside cold windows fogged up by early rain. The two of them were also in different divisions again, which made it harder for them to talk during school. They'd steal glances through the open doorway when they passed outside each other's classroom. Sometimes, they'd sit in the canteen during breaks with two glasses of lemonade laid out in front of them and share their lunch.

After school, Dhruv would go to Aanya's house and help her mother arrange washed dishes or clean up the living room. He would then play board games with Aanya while they ate evening snacks and watched TV together. They'd drop a chit into their bowls every now and then. Aanya would write some of her favourite words, and Dhruv would put down the names of songs or a lyric from one of his favourite tracks. That year, he was listening to a lot of Bryan Adams from a CD his uncle had gifted him and some Linkin Park songs a friend had introduced him to. He would keep singing the songs to himself, but Aanya never seemed to like any of them. She would sit in a corner at her teal desk and write drafts in her book of poems while Dhruv

Thirteen

danced around the room playing air guitar with his eyes closed. This would continue until Aanya's mother would call out to them and scold them for not studying enough. Dhruv would plot his escape at the sound of her call and run outside to play basketball with others, while Aanya would stay back and study by herself. The same routine would repeat itself every day until the weekend rolled over.

On weekends, Aanya's father would come back home after travelling all week. He would be greeted with long embraces and laughter and would take the family out to eat, or bring DVDs for them to watch at home. They would lay curled up on the bed on movie nights, munching on popcorn and drinking multiple bottles of Coke. Sometimes, during the evenings, Aanya's father would leave the house for a walk and return with a garland of white flowers for Aanya's mother to wear in her hair. He would tiptoe over to the kitchen and slowly tie the garland around the bun on her head, feeling each strand out with his fingers. They would then play old Hindi songs in the living room and dance together. Aanya would hear the music and join in, and the three would end up dancing and singing until it was dark outside and their stomachs were rumbling for dinner. Aanya's father would cook a big meal for them before packing his suitcase for his Monday morning flight. One Sunday evening though, a few days before Aanya's thirteenth birthday, he left to buy a garland of flowers, but never returned. Walking in a narrow lane crowded by cars packed against one another, he collapsed with a small pain in his chest and didn't make it to the hospital in time.

～

'Are you still using your dictionary?' Dhruv asked Aanya as they stood hidden behind their bus in the school parking lot. Their fingers were interlaced underneath Dhruv's lunchbox as they shared leftovers from it.

'Yes. When papa comes back, he'll ask me about what I learnt.'

'What's the last word you learnt?' Dhruv continued weakly.

'W-i-t-h-e-r. Wither. Why do flowers wither away so easily?' They both cried.

'I can't believe this is your last day,' Dhruv said as he wiped his face.

'It's okay,' Aanya replied, clutching his hand. 'If we promise to remember each other, we will.'

Aanya left to live with her grandparents after that. The drive was only a couple of hours away, yet she never came back, and no one knew exactly where her family lived. The first Sunday of August came after she moved, and it was Friendship Day. Before she left, Aanya had managed to leave a friendship band for Dhruv with his mother. He cried alone in his room as he crumpled the bright red ribbon into his fist. Small threads had already started peeling off from its ends.

Thirteen

Ages: 24, 24

'So, you're here to finally sell the house.'

'Dhruv …'

'Aanya.' A long pause ensued with neither of them finding the words. 'I saw the movers taking away things and recognised most of them,' Dhruv finally said as he tried to place Aanya in the backdrop of the pale dove sky. A red construction crane moved objects around in the distance.

'Wow, it's been so long. How—how are you? What do you do now?' She tilted her head to one side and brushed her shoulder against her face.

'I'm your standard, boring Indian engineer. What about you? Have you become a published writer already?'

'A writer?' she forced a laugh. 'No, I work in investment banking.'

'Ooh, turns out you are smarter than me after all.'

'I'm sorry?' She lightly scratched some parts of her hands.

'You remember how we used to debate about who's smarter?'

'Come on. It's not like that.' Her voice overlapped with the sound of the first drops of rain scattering around them.

'You've changed so much. It's like I'm meeting a whole new person,' he said without looking at her. The construction crane in the distance dropped a set of steel girders with a loud crash.

'You're right, I have. It was good to see you, Dhruv. I should get going.' Aanya's disc earrings swayed with the wind as she spoke, and Dhruv followed their dull silver glow with a soft gaze.

'Leaving already?'

'I'm quite busy,' she said as the rain picked up and it started to pour.

'You could come home if you wanted to.'

'No, it's—'

'Come on! Let's run inside at least?' he said as he turned and ran towards his building. Aanya followed him somewhat involuntarily. They both looked at each other and smiled as they ran.

'You should come home,' Dhruv said once they were both away from the rain.

'No, thank you. I'll just wait—'

'I could make you something warm and we could talk.'

'Okay,' she sighed. 'Just for some time.'

As Aanya sat in Dhruv's room, she realised that it had changed a lot from what she remembered, with only sparse remnants of the past. An old Spalding basketball on the floor, a jar full of friendship bands and a class photograph from the only year they were in the same division leaning against it, notebooks with brown covers stapled onto them and a colourful pile of Enid Blyton books that he had never read, all of which she had borrowed at some point.

'You never read any of these,' Aanya smirked, pointing to the pile as Dhruv walked in with two mugs of Bournvita.

Thirteen

'I did read them eventually. You wouldn't know because you weren't here.'

'Right ...' she said softly.

'I'm sorry. How have you been all these years?' Dhruv asked as he set the two mugs down between them.

'I've been good. I got by school and college somehow and managed to get a job that I love. Worked straight out of college and I'm engaged now.'

'To whom?'

'My boyfriend from college. His name's Rajat. We've been together for five years and we're getting married next spring.'

'In my mind, you're still in eighth grade with me.' Dhruv placed his knees against his chest and leaned against the wall behind him.

'Please tell me I don't still look like an eighth grader.'

'That's not what I meant,' he said, and Aanya laughed to herself.

'What about you? Any girlfriends?' she asked.

'Not really. There was a girl I saw in college for a while. We went on a few dates and connected well, but I always had cold feet about going any further. We're still good friends and maybe that's what we're supposed to be,' he said as he stirred his glass. 'Bournvita used to be your favourite drink,' he smiled.

'I had it all the time, didn't I? I try to avoid it now.' They drew a few more sips, warming up their faces and spent the next few minutes in silence. Dhruv scratched his calves while Aanya watched the sky through the window behind him. The shadow of the curtain strings tried to touch her face every now and then.

'The rain's eased again. Maybe I should get going,' Aanya said after a while as she picked up her purse.

'Will you come to school with me?' Dhruv asked as the words escaped him like a wisp of cold air. He placed his empty mug carefully on the ledge behind him.

'After all these years … I don't know. I'm not really a sad nostalgia kind of person.'

'But aren't you curious about what's changed after all this time?'

'I'm not a big fan of revisiting things. I've realised that it's best to just let them be.' Dhruv stared at the white wall behind Aanya. 'But I'm planning to take the train back home,' she started again. 'School's on the way to the station. So maybe we could drop by for a bit.'

'Let me quickly get an umbrella and some other things,' Dhruv replied excitedly as he got up and shuffled through his cupboard to pack an old shoulder bag. 'Let's leave,' he said with a smile.

Dhruv and Aanya sat in a rickshaw and directed the driver about where to go. As the rickshaw started moving, Dhruv looked out at the route he had taken every day for four years, from ninth grade until graduation. The same rickshaw ride, always exactly twelve minutes long. And despite the short commute, he had never reached school on time.

Thirteen

'Come to think of it, we've never sat in a rickshaw together before. That's so strange,' Aanya said as the wind threw her hair in a flutter.

'We only ever did bus rides together,' Dhruv replied as he watched the fare on the electronic meter increase. Leftover raindrops clinging to the windshield gradually slipped off as foggy traffic signals passed by outside. The morning rush of the city seemed to be falling apart.

A few minutes later, they stopped opposite their school, and Aanya settled the fare before Dhruv could even reach into his pocket. The rickshaw driver returned some change and slowly drove away, revealing an unbroken view of the school building. Flowerpots hung on both sides of the lamps that ran along the street. A balloon seller passed by Dhruv and Aanya as they tried to cross over to the other side.

'What now?' Aanya asked once they were in front of the school's main gate.

'The security guard won't let us through. But we can sneak in through the side gate.'

'Absolutely not, Dhruv! We are going to get into so much trouble.'

'Don't worry, that gate's always locked and no one's there. I've done this before,' he said as he started running towards the side gate. Aanya followed him helplessly.

'Stop running around like a kid,' she said once he had stopped and lightly slapped his shoulder.

'We don't have a lot of time,' he said as he climbed over a rusty blue gate and jumped off to enter the school.

'I'm not doing this.'

'Are you scared?' he asked as his feet crushed some of the pink flowers scattered all around.

'No, I'm not scared.'

'Then prove it,' he smirked.

'You're so childish,' she complained as she climbed her way in.

'Okay, let's go now, Ms Grown-up!'

'Yes, sir,' Aanya replied as she smiled facing Dhruv's back and lightly shook her head. His hair no longer grazed the seam of his collar like it always used to after summer breaks.

The two of them walked by empty basketball courts and a muddy football field. Some kids in the distance were busy playing with the family of geese that lived inside the school. The holiday vacancy that ran over the place gave it a strange mid-afternoon silence. Dhruv and Aanya climbed up some steps by the accounts office and tiptoed their way inside the main building.

They entered a dimly lit passage of locked classrooms and old staircases that they would use to bunk periods. 'Do you want to go to our floor?' Dhruv asked in a whisper and Aanya nodded her head in agreement.

They went up a slope and crossed a bridge that connected two separately constructed halves of the school. A long, gradually arching corridor emerged on the other side. Dhruv stared at the

Thirteen

large digital clock at the end of the corridor that read out the time in glowing red numbers.

'This one's open,' Aanya said as she pushed the door of an unlocked classroom and stepped inside. Dhruv followed her and found a piece of chalk along the blackboard on his way in. 'Pay attention, Aanya!' he said as he broke the white stick into two and threw the smaller half at her.

'Come, sit,' Aanya replied, brushing the chalk stain away and taking up a place in the back row. Dhruv climbed over some chairs and sat on the table in front of her. A chart on polar satellites was pinned on to a soft board behind them.

'Are you sure you don't want to go up a floor to the eighth grade?'

'No, this is good.'

'You know, after you left, I was sure I'd become the house prefect. If you were around, I wouldn't have had a chance.'

'That's not true. But why didn't you?'

'My grades weren't good enough,' he laughed. 'But I wouldn't change what happened. School was the best time of my life. I keep wanting to go back to it.'

'Doesn't that make you stuck in the past? Romanticising time gone by like that …' she said softly.

'Partly you're right. I guess it's because back then we could be anyone. Now we've to live this life of dwindling possibilities.'

'I like who you've become.'

'But you don't know me anymore.' Dhruv's hair fluttered as bits of cold air blew in towards him from a partially open window. 'This is a little selfish, Aanya, but why didn't you ever try to talk to me again? Why did you forget about me?'

'I didn't forget about you,' she said as she shifted in her seat and the chair's metal leg screeched against the white tiled floor.

'I felt abandoned after you left and never spoke to me again.'

'I'm sorry. You know what it was like for me.'

Dhruv slumped down onto an adjacent chair and placed his head down on the desk. Aanya moved her chair beside him and stroked his hair affectionately. She held him as she lay her face down next to his. Faint sunlight brushed against the fringes of her face.

'You could've told me somehow that you were coming,' Dhruv said as he sat up and playfully punched Aanya's shoulder.

'I was scared about facing you after so long.'

'You're silly. That's why I always said you weren't smarter than me.'

'Maybe I'm not.' Aanya smiled as she sniffled into her sleeve.

'Do you still read your dictionary every day?'

'No, I don't. What's the point of learning all those big words anyway?' The sound of her voice seemed to stretch on for a long time.

'I'll show you something,' Dhruv said as he reached into the bottom of his bag and placed his fishbowl in front of Aanya.

'It's sweet that you still keep these.' She excitedly pulled a chit out from the bowl at random.

'*I wanna love you* by Akon,' she read out slowly.

Thirteen

'Don't judge me,' Dhruv said, embarrassed.

'Definitely judging you right now,' she laughed loudly. The two of them took turns taking out chits one by one. They ran through several of them until Aanya pulled one out and paused for a moment.

'*Thirteen* by Big Star. Do you want to listen to it?' she asked as she unlocked her phone and played the song at a low volume. Without realising it, Dhruv started singing along, and a few lines later, Aanya joined him. They giggled as they took turns fumbling over lyrics that they had forgotten.

'My voice has changed a lot,' Dhruv said once the song had ended.

'Your voice is still the same,' Aanya replied with a wide smile, and Dhruv felt the sun's gaze soften over them. 'I'm sorry, Dhruv,' she continued as she stared at a shelf full of small notebooks in the corner of the class.

'I'm sorry too, Aanya,' he replied.

'You know, Ma still misses you.'

'Does she?' He looked directly at her.

'Yes, very much. You used to come home every day.' Aanya looked back at him.

'I didn't want to go back to my house.'

'I know. I remember how much we cried together when you told me your parents were separating.'

'Long time ago now,' he smiled at her as he made a tiny paper plane out of one of the chits. 'Do you remember? You taught me how to make one of these.'

Song of the Day

'Papa taught me,' she smiled as she took a chit and started folding it.

The two of them made several paper planes and flew them all around the room. Half an hour later, they lay in a mess of planes. Dark clouds had once again started to adorn the dusky sky outside the classroom's clear windows.

'We've spent so many years apart. But I still feel this sense of familiarity with you. Even though you're so different from what I remember, I feel like I know you,' Aanya said as they stood against the back wall of the classroom.

'Here, I want you to keep this. I can never forget how sad you were when you lost yours,' Dhruv said as he reached into his bag and handed Aanya their class photograph.

'But this belongs to you,' she protested.

'I've had it for long enough now.'

They smiled at each other, and Aanya kept the photograph safely in her purse. Then they collected the planes on the floor and put them back into the bowl. Dhruv stored the bowl in his bag, and they left the classroom and went down a staircase that led to an exit. As they walked towards the main gate, they passed by the empty parking lot where they would always board a bus back home together.

'I'll come with you to the station,' Dhruv said once they were by the street again.

'Okay,' Aanya replied as she glanced back at their school. A weak drizzle was falling over them, and tiny droplets of rain stuck onto their clothes. They found a rickshaw and within a

Thirteen

few minutes, they reached the station. Dhruv paid the driver the full amount due, and they headed towards the departures section.

As Dhruv and Aanya walked under an umbrella through the crowded train station, a strong gust came but Dhruv's hands remained steady. They found the correct platform number and stood facing the train scheduled to leave.

'This feels like your last day at school,' Dhruv said quietly to himself as his words almost got crushed under the station's noise.

'We're much happier today,' Aanya replied with half a smile. She thought about how all those years ago she'd always wished that Dhruv was in her class so that they could dance together during their annual function. Parents would come to watch their children perform in an open-air amphitheatre by the canteen. The stage, lit up by old yellow light bulbs, was always newly repainted by the art department. Hundreds of grey plastic chairs would be lined up for the audience, where every kid would search for someone from their family. The simple joy of finding a familiar face in a sea full of strangers.

'Do you think we could dance together one day?' Aanya asked as she looked away at an incoming train slowing itself down.

'Maybe, if you practise enough,' Dhruv replied as they exchanged a brief glance and started laughing at each other. He wondered how much he and Aanya had forgotten over their time apart. The dull, silver glow of the past had become distant and faint, and they could no longer place those childhood memories like they once could. Those years had passed by like a sea of balloons drifting away, and without realising it, they had crossed over to the other side.

'If you ever come to my side of town, call me,' Aanya said all of a sudden as she stepped out of the umbrella and turned her head back towards Dhruv.

'I will. Bye, Aanya,' he said with a smile.

'Bye, Dhruv,' she happily replied.

～

Ages: 12, 12

'Make a birthday wish,' Dhruv said to Aanya as they sat under a banyan tree.

'I don't know what to wish for,' she replied.

'Come on. It could be anything you want.'

Aanya thought carefully for a while and then tugged lightly at Dhruv's shirt, motioning him to close his eyes. Once both their eyes were closed, she locked her fingers with Dhruv's and tightly held his hand.

'If we prayed really hard, do you think we would always stay together?'

～

The Little Things You Do

Faiz leaned against a tree as figures of people strolled by him in early morning attire and small, whole-hearted laughs. He waited for a while before a girl with big round glasses, wearing a full-sleeved top, slowly walked towards him. He glanced at her as a flower, dislodged by a sudden breeze, danced past her face and brushed against her shoulder.

'Hi, Meera,' Faiz called out as he started walking towards her. A momentary rush of warmth came upon him as he slipped out of the shade.

'I'm sorry. Were you waiting for long?' Meera asked as she held one of her ears apologetically. Faiz shook his head and smiled back at her.

'Let's walk?' he suggested.

Song of the Day

'You know, it's my first time coming to a happy street,' Meera said as she took a sideward glance at Faiz. The sun gleamed from the outlines of his face.

'I've been here a few times. I love how they close the street to cars, and we can use it for anything we want to do. Sometimes I wish they would shut the entire city down like this for us,' he said as he stretched his arms wide and spun in a circle.

'How is that going to work?'

'I don't know. I just want it to happen once. Is that a lot to ask for?' Faiz looked at Meera with a soft gaze.

'Not at all,' she giggled.

'Anyway, is there anything you want to do on your first time? They have a Zumba session!'

'Let's just continue walking for a while,' Meera replied as they headed towards the southern end of the street. A line of school buses parked idly stood on the side of the road. Faiz and Meera waved out to familiar faces every now and then and made plans to meet soon; eat at a Subway together or hang out in the park nearby sometime.

'How do you think you did in the board exams?' Meera asked after some time as she cupped her hands together and blew puffs of cold air into them. A group of kids was blowing bubbles in the sky and chasing after them in loud giggles.

'No idea. I just want this break to go on forever and the results to never come out.'

'It's all anyone could talk about all this time, and now, all of a sudden, it's behind us. Isn't that a little disorienting?'

'I find it quite relaxing,' Faiz replied cheerfully, hop-skipping as he walked.

'You're never going to change, are you?' Meera laughed.

'I won't! By the way, did you hear? Basu ma'am is retiring.'

'I couldn't believe it at first. We're going to be her last batch of students.'

'People from my class are thinking about going to meet her.'

'I'm sure she'll like that,' Meera said as she stopped at the entrance of an old plaza. Leftover ash from a small fire, ignited by someone the previous night, swirled along the narrow footpath. Faiz and Meera stood there for a while as they leaned against a rusted old handrail and took sidelong glances at each other.

'Remind me to buy cello tape. I'm making a scrapbook,' Meera said as their eyes suddenly met.

'For what?' Faiz asked.

'I'm collecting pictures from the last two years of school. It's my project for these three months.' She turned away from him as she finished. Her cheeks were concealed by strands of her hair, and Faiz wondered whether they had always been this long.

'That sounds like a lot of work. Will you show it to me once you're done?' he asked.

'As if you won't be the first person to see,' Meera replied playfully. 'Faiz, what are you planning to do during this break?'

'I think I'm going to play cricket or football all day. And we'll meet, of course.'

'We will?' she asked and paused for a moment. 'You know, I've been reading this book called *Tuesdays with Morrie* and I'm loving it.'

'Can you lend it to me when you're done?'

'Of course, but you didn't even ask what it's about. Will you actually read it?' she smirked at him.

'If you love it, then I'll try,' he said with a smile as he pulled her cheeks affectionately. She stepped back with a big smile that waned somewhat quickly, like icicles that had been kissed by the sun.

'Faiz?'

'Yes, Meera?'

'Do you want to make a deal with me?' Meera's gaze held a faraway look.

'A deal?'

'For this one hour or so today that we're together here, we can tell each other anything. No judgements.'

'Sure, but—'

'Don't ask me why,' she said in a rushed manner.

'Okay, I won't,' he smiled at her.

'Can we go into the plaza?' Meera asked, and Faiz nodded in agreement. They walked towards the entrance and down a set of stairs that led to long forgotten shops and old tuition centres still clinging onto youth.

'We've attended classes here for two years. Do you think we'll ever come back to this place a few years from now?' Faiz asked as he thought about how he and his friends had spent every evening after tuitions together, sitting on parked car bonnets and talking for hours at times.

'I would want to. But we forget what we want so easily.'

'Does something make you feel that way?'

'It's just … I wish we could be stationary. Everything always moves two steps ahead of us. I'm scared sometimes that I'll fall apart.' Meera's voice felt fragile, like a withered leaf that falls off at the first sensation of touch.

'What do you mean?'

'You know, when we had our study break before the board exams, I used to spend a lot of time staring at the sky. Everything was so beautiful. I wanted to be outside so badly every day. It seemed like the most beautiful time in my life. And now—' She broke off all of a sudden.

'And now?'

'Now that time is gone and the sky has changed, I can no longer see things the same way.'

'I'm a little confused.

'I'm sorry, I'm not making much sense,' Meera replied as she looked straight at Faiz. Her eyes seemed like brown ovals of clay shaped delicately to resemble the moon.

'Do you want to sit at our place and talk?' he asked as he rubbed her head affectionately with his palm.

Faiz and Meera went through a faintly lit corridor and made their way to a quiet corner of the plaza. The sound of their footsteps hung in the air as they sat down on an abandoned staircase. A dark emptiness lay around them, blocking out the bright morning and the low buzz of people outside.

'Are you okay?' Faiz asked as he put an arm around Meera's shoulder and leaned in close to her.

'Yes.' She clenched her fist tightly, as if she was trying to cling on to the air between her palms.

'Then why are you scared?'

'I'm scared we'll grow up one day.'

'And why does that scare you?' Faiz asked as he gently held her hand.

'So much that we don't realise will fade within. I've seen it with my sister. So many of her closest friends from school are no longer in touch with her.'

'You're my oldest friend … If that happened, I would only cry.' He tried to hold her as tightly as he could.

'We keep getting older. And we keep losing people we adore. Sure, we can promise to stay in touch, but how many promises will we keep?'

'I'll always be true to you. Will you always be true to me?'

'I will, Faiz. I've carried this fear with me since the last day of school and I've only been able to share it with you. I'm at ease when you're around. I don't want that to change.'

'There's something I've been keeping to myself too,' Faiz said as he touched the back of his neck. 'My grandmother passed away during our board exams. And I just couldn't bring myself to tell anyone. It was such an important time for all of us. I didn't want to burden anyone.'

'I am so sorry. I don't know what to … what to say. How are you?' She reached for his shoulder.

'I'm okay,' Faiz nodded to himself. 'In some ways, I feel like I've crossed over to a new place where I am someone else. I can never return and yet I've found a certain happiness.' He fell silent for a moment. 'Maybe it's gratitude that I knew who my grandmother was; what helped her find beauty in life.'

'Is that what it is? That keeps people going despite what they lose.'

'Maybe,' Faiz replied. 'There's not a lot that we can control, but I hope as time passes, we find that our strongest bonds always remain within us.'

'One day, if I feel like I'm alone, can I call you?'

'I'll call you every afternoon,' he replied. Meera smiled widely after that. A wind chime hanging above a nearby classroom swayed gently and gave off a sweet ring through the air.

'What will you remember the most about this year?' she asked as she crudely rubbed her eyes.

'The time when we played a water fight in school and ended up getting sent to the coordinator's office.' They both laughed. 'You?'

'That night during annual day when the teachers weren't letting us leave after our performance. You jumped out the first-floor window, but came back because you realised you had left without me.'

Song of the Day

'That was such a bad idea! I got into a lot of trouble when I came back. They made me stand on a kindergarten chair with my hands raised for a long time.'

'You never told me how they let you go finally.'

'You really want to know?' he asked, and Meera nodded with muted mischief on her face. 'They made me write a letter to the principal saying I jumped from a window because I was worried about not finding a rickshaw at night.' Meera burst into laughter as Faiz tried his best to shrug it off. Their voices echoed in the hollowness of the space around them.

'Faiz, will you sing for me?' Meera asked as she grew quiet again.

'Of course,' he replied and thought for a while before singing *The Little Things You Do* by Mikey McCleary. Meera placed her head on his shoulder and hummed along.

'I'll remember today by this song,' she whispered once they had stopped singing.

'Me too,' he whispered back. They sat there for a while staring at the trails of light that broke in every now and then from the world outside.

'Faiz?' Meera said all of a sudden as she placed a small kiss on his cheek.

'Yes … yes, Meera?'

'Will you split a Cadbury with me?'

~